handwritten: De... & are blesse... (You all in our prayers) ...ydene "Rae" Brandt-Thompson

Saint's Hospital

The Soul Searchers Series

By Clydene R. Brandt

PublishAmerica
Baltimore

ISBN: 1-4241-0089-5
PUBLISHED BY PUBLISHAMERICA, LLLP
www.publishamerica.com
Baltimore

Printed in the United States of America

This book is dedicated to the Glory of God, and to my brother-in-law and sister, Rev. and Mrs. F.D. Cody, who have gone on to see God and *all of his angels* in a heaven that is indescribable. Their influence is living on in many, many lives. They would have been so proud to share in this project.

Acknowledgments

Thank you to all the friends and family that supported me during the writing of this book. To Faye Sanders and David McLain who are true "encouragers" and would not let me give up; to Pat Mason and Donese Copeland, who helped me proofread and edit the book; to my two critique groups, Novel Ideas and Wordwrights; to my courageous, brave friend, Ranelle Newport; to my Webmaster, John (Jack) Passarella, through whose genius, wit, and patience proved to be the calm in a number of storms; last, not least, I thank my family, Jay, Belinda, David, Valerie, Stephanie, Megan and Heather. The privilege is mine in loving you.

—*C.R.Brandt*

Prologue

"Are not all angels ministering spirits sent to serve those who will inherit salvation?"

Hebrews 1:14

Chapter One

He slammed on his brakes, jumped out of his pickup, and rushed to the wrecked mass of metal, that a few minutes earlier had been a new, bright, red sedan. John Cabe saw the woman go off the road. He was about one-half mile behind her when it happened. She had passed him, flying by at over ninety miles per hour.

They were on a two-lane road that John traveled daily. His ranch was a few miles back and he knew there were too many curves and hills to be going that fast. Then, it happened. The woman's car went out of control and swerved to the edge, careening up-and-over. John watched it, as it turned around in the air, like a bird that forgot its flight path. It was unreal, similar to seeing a movie in slow motion. Then, he heard the screech of the landing and saw the car land upside down on the pavement.

"Good Lord, look at that!" John shouted.

He couldn't believe what he was seeing. He whispered a short, quick prayer for the woman he had seen and anyone else who might be involved.

As he ran closer to the wreckage, he thought he saw someone

move. He had parked his pickup on the opposite side of the road and he rushed across to see if anyone survived. He looked through the broken front window where the driver, a young woman, was slumped over the wheel. Her auburn hair mingled with the darkness of blood and John noticed a small fire inside the car. He had to get her out of the wreckage before the fire traveled to the gas tank and exploded.

"Blast!" he said, as he tried to open the bent car door.

It's jammed. I need a crowbar. God, help me. Don't panic...

He remembered the tools in his pickup and raced back to it, scattered thoughts churning in his mind.

Hurry...faster! She's unconscious. She'll burn to death unless I hurry.

He found the crowbar, and as he reached her door again, he placed it into the metal, dug his boots into the ground and pulled on the front door with all of the strength he had. It opened!

Quick, get her seatbelt undone. Watch out! Don't hurt her. Gently...

John grabbed her under each arm, and pulled her away from the wreckage. One of the sleeves on her dress was scorched from the inside fire. The fabric was still smoldering and some of it had melted into her flesh. The right side of her face was burned.

"I should have gotten to you sooner. It's okay, Babe, I've got you now."

He swatted away the remaining cinders from her dress and half-carried, half-dragged her onto the concrete highway.

Come on, John. I have to get across the road and into that ditch.

The fumes from a gasoline leak were pungent. John knew he had to get them further away. The car was smoking now, and flames could be seen multiplying and leaping up and over the engine! Using all the strength he had, John picked the woman up and carried her to a small ravine on the other side of the road.

He laid her down on hard dirt, peppered with stiffened dry weeds, as he heard the car *groan* behind him. John turned to see it explode into bright orange flames and thick black smoke. Pieces of glass and metal were fired, like projectiles—up in the air and over the highway, where John huddled with the woman.

He tried to cover her body with his own. As he glanced back at the car, a sharp pain hit his temple. It burrowed through like a bullet—through the skin and just above his eye. John's face burned like fire!

He tried to bury the woman and himself into the safety of the dirt below them, but it was too late…

His vision was fading and soon, he couldn't see anything. John Cabe was *BLIND!*

The driver of a sixteen-wheeler approached the top of the hill and just over the crest, saw the smoke and wreckage. There was very little left of the auto except for blackened, twisted metal. He quickly radioed for the closest sheriff's office and requested help and an ambulance.

No one could have made it through that, but where are they?

He noticed a white pickup, parked directly across the road from the crash. It didn't have a dent on it.

Someone must have stopped to help.

He slowed his truck and pulled over in front of the pickup. The driver climbed out and surveyed the crash site. He didn't see any other cars involved, just these two. He wondered what happened to both of the drivers and any passengers. He couldn't see anyone from where he stood but, at that moment, he heard a pain-filled groan from the opposite side of the road.

He started walking toward the noise when he saw them. In the ditch by the shoulder of the road was a man, whose faced was covered with blood. At his side was a young woman who appeared to be unconscious. As the truck driver got closer, he saw the burns on the woman's arms and face. The man was writhing in pain.

"Hang in there, buddy," he said, as he scrambled down into the small ravine.

Another groan surfaced.

"I've contacted the sheriff. They're sending an ambulance."

The man was alive, but he wasn't certain about the woman. He tried to find a pulse on her, but couldn't pick up any from her limp wrist or her neck.

"I've got a first aid kit in my truck. I'll be right back."

The driver ran back to his rig to get the kit and a blanket. He remembered a water bottle in the front, and grabbed that too, and then rushed back to the two victims. He wondered if the ambulance would reach them in time.

As he returned to the ravine, the trucker heard the faint sound of a siren in the distance. He knelt down and told the man he had water. As he put the water bottle close to the man's mouth, John Cabe grabbed for it, along with the driver's arm.

"My eyes!" he gasped. "I can't see anything."

The truck driver saw a large piece of bloody metal laying beside the man. Multi-sized pieces of broken glass were sticking out of his face, like a cactus. One piece of glass had landed close to his eye. The driver couldn't risk removing it. He covered the man with a blanket.

"Just lie still and don't move," he said. "The ambulance will be here any minute."

The woman looked lifeless, but the driver started C.P.R. on her. Under his rough exterior, the truck driver was a praying man, and he knew if anyone needed it, it was these two human beings.

The sheriff's car pulled up next to the rig. The Sheriff climbed down the ravine.

"Where's the ambulance? I don't know if these two can hold on much longer," the trucker shouted.

He watched, as the Sheriff grabbed his mobile phone and called the hospital.

"Where's that ambulance? This is Sheriff Biggs. We need one out here on Highway 180 immediately. There's been a bad wreck and a fire!"

The Sheriff, still on the phone, removed his sunglasses, looked to the East, and saw another vehicle heading their way. He heard the wail of the ambulance.

John Cabe woke up, feeling cold, damp bandages covering his eyes and forehead. Everything was dark. John couldn't see anything or hear anyone. He moved his hand down to his side and felt what he guessed were starched sheets. He was in a hospital bed. He knew that, but he didn't remember why.

John tried to feel his forehead with his other hand, but felt tubing connected to his arm and realized he must be hooked up to some I.V.'s. As he tried to lift his head from the pillow, his head pounded and then he remembered...the woman and the crash! In the back of his mind, he wondered if she had died.

He yelled out.

"Hey! Is anyone around?"

John assumed he was in a hospital, but he heard no sound at all. He yelled again, louder this time.

"Hey! Is anyone out there?"

"Good boy!"

A male voice was speaking, and footsteps were coming closer to him.

"We were all praying you'd wake up soon. You've been asleep for days, Mr. Cabe. It's a good sign—you're waking up. I'm Dr. Martin, John."

The physician put his hand into John's hand. It was a strong grip and John Cabe latched onto it as if a life preserver had just been thrown to him. It was comforting to feel another human being.

"Where am I?" he asked the physician.

"You're in Saints Hospital, Mr. Cabe, just outside Clarksville. You've been here for almost six days. Do you remember anything about the automobile crash that brought you here?"

"I remember a woman…an explosion. I tried to get her out of the wreckage before the car exploded."

John couldn't believe he had slept for six days! He tried to process what the doctor was saying to him.

"What happened to her? What happened to the woman?"

"She's here, Mr. Cabe. She's in-patient in our Burn Unit. It's pretty serious, but I think she'll make it, thanks to you."

"My eyes? What about my eyes, Dr. Martin?"

John didn't want to think about what the doctor might tell him. In the darkness, the fear was beginning to surround him.

Dr. Anthony Martin looked down at his patient. He wasn't certain that the man would comprehend everything, but he tried to explain. He would go over it again with him later, when he was stronger.

"You've come back from a long sleep, Mr. Cabe. We believe you were hit in the head by a heavy piece of metal from the wreckage. It was laying beside you when the truck driver and the sheriff found you. You had a bad concussion.

"There was also a piece of glass that was wedged near your eye, although it didn't enter it. We're hoping your eyesight will return, but we just aren't sure when. As soon as you feel a little better, you're going to have to undergo a few more tests for us. That will tell us more."

The physician tried to sound calm. His patient was making sense with his questions and there were no signs of seizure activity—that was a good sign.

"In the meantime, Mr. Cabe," he continued, "we want you to try and rest. Here. Here's the buzzer for your nurse."

The doctor covered John's hand with his own, letting him feel the buzzer.

"I'm going to pin it on the pillow, where you can find it. You call us if you need anything. I know this is going to be a difficult time, but I'm here to help you through it."

John's mind was spinning.

What if my sight doesn't return? How am I going to function? I'm a pilot—a computer engineer. I just lost my entire livelihood...

He was beginning to panic, and his head felt as if it was going to explode.

The physician recognized his patient's plight, and ordered some pain medication.

"I'll get you something for that headache. Try not to worry. It's to be expected."

Dr. Martin asked John if he could call some family or friends for him, and told him that he would explain everything later, in more detail, to make certain he understood.

John Cabe thought of his friends in California. He wanted to talk to Nick Stewart or to Mac. He gave the doctor their names, and Nick's phone number.

It wasn't long before he was given an injection. The medication began its pleasant journey through his system. As the pain eased, John felt a well-being that he knew was coming from the narcotic. He drifted off to sleep, with the doctor still holding on to his hand. John could hear the physician praying.

Chapter Two

John awoke to the sound of a feminine voice, urging him to wake up. He felt her hand on his, gently shaking it.

"Mr. Cabe? You have a telephone call. It's a Mr. Nicholas Stewart. Do you feel like taking it? I can ask him to phone you back, if you don't."

John's memory was fuzzy, but he remembered he *had* to talk to Nick. He still couldn't see anything but darkness, but he tried to reach the nurse's arm.

"Please. I want to speak to him. Where's the phone?"

"I'll bring it to you. Don't worry. I won't leave for long. I'll be right back."

She patted his hand, but when she left, he felt the world go away. He wanted to cry out. He was a grown man, known for being pretty tough, but this? No one would ever have expected this. For the first time in many months, he was afraid!

The nurse came back into the room. He could hear her footsteps on the tile floor. She set the telephone next to him on the bed, and then held the receiver to his ear, while he placed his own hand over hers.

"Nick?" he called out. "Nick, I think I need you, man."

The voice on the other end of the line appeared to calm him. The nurse watched him, as his breathing slowed, and she felt sorry for him. He was a handsome man, with reddish-brown hair, over six feet tall. He was tan from the sun and hard work had formed calluses on his large hands. She knew that he was afraid.

To get through this, he was going to need all the friends that he had.

Nick Stewart took the phone call from the Arizona Hospital. He couldn't believe what had happened to his friend. John Cabe was not only a friend—he used to be Nick Stewart's pilot, his right arm. John told him that he was blinded in an accident.

Nick heard the fear in his friend's voice as he asked for help, and Nick tried to calm him. He told John that he would find a doctor, a surgeon, or any specialist he might need and he told him not to worry.

"I'll be there in the morning, John. I'll phone Mac for you. Please, John, try to rest. We'll work out something. I promise. I'll help you. You know that."

As Nick Stewart hung up the phone, he said a quick prayer for his friend and then ordered a helicopter. He called Mac Timmons, another of John's close friend, and asked him if he could fly with him to Arizona in the morning.

Nick only had to say that John needed both of them and Mac Timmons didn't hesitate. He said he was coming with Nick.

Nicholas Stewart—The nurse knew his name. Who didn't? He was famous—an actor—and a hero of sort. So, Mr. Cabe's a friend of his?

The nurse tried to remember what she had read in a newspaper article sometime back. Stewart and his friends had caught the leader of some terrorist group some months back. She had read about the trial of the man they caught. He was sentenced to death. Nick Stewart, his wife Alexandra, and John Cabe had squelched a plot that threatened several countries.

She didn't remember all of the details, but she realized now, who her patient was. John Cabe was a hero, although he would probably never admit it to anyone. What was he doing in Arizona?

This man—to have been blinded in a freak accident…

The nurse closed her eyes for a moment, seeing the blackness that was now her patient's fate. She said a prayer that he wouldn't be able to discern what she was thinking. He would never want pity—not this man.

As John Cabe finished his conversation, he handed the phone receiver back to her—this nameless angel that he couldn't see.

"He's coming," John said to her. "My friend's coming to be with me."

"I'm so glad, Mr. Cabe. Can I get you anything else? I've been asked to stay with you for awhile."

She handed him a small glass of ice water and a straw and, as she put his hand around it, she guided it to his lips. As he swallowed the cold liquid, he felt again for her hand. It was a lifeline to him. He covered her small hands with his own, feeling her soft skin on the hard, cool glass.

"Are you hungry, Mr. Cabe? You've had an I.V. for days. It would be good if you could eat something—soup or something soft at first. Perhaps, something to drink?"

John appreciated her kindness in the tone of her voice.

"Soup? That might be Okay. I may need some help."

"Of course. I'm going to get that ordered. I'll be right back. Oh, and Mr. Cabe...?"

"Yes?"

"I'll have Joseph come in, and he can assist you and help you bathe."

She's being diplomatic. She must have sensed I'd never agree to a woman undressing me and bathing me—at least, not like this.

John reflected on his life before this happened to him. Women always wanted to do things for him, and he always counted on being persuasive. He liked women and he enjoyed flirting with them. He relished the fact that his friends thought of him as a *lady's man*. Now, anything they did for him would be—out of pity. His life, as he knew it, had just disappeared.

His fingers dug into the palms of his own hands as he thought about this, leaving red indentations on his palms. He was so angry. This was so unfair! If there was a God, why would He allow this? He slammed his fists onto the bed, twisting the I.V. around them—and he swore!

"Damn you! Why? Why did you do this to me?"

John Cabe cursed his unknown God—the God his own mother had loved so much—the God people thanked for good things—and he wept until he could weep no more.

The male nurse, Joseph, had walked into the room, carrying a washbasin. John realized that the man was in the room before he finished his tirade against God.

"Who is it? Who's there?" he yelled out.

"It's Joseph, sir…uh, I've come to assist. Ms. Maureen told me to help you."

"Oh, sorry."

John sighed.

So, the nurse's name is Maureen, and this is Joseph, come to bathe me.

He had little strength left. He was so weary, but John asked Joseph to help him sit up. What he really wanted to do was to stand up and throw things, but he knew that was impossible right now. He wanted to know where *everything* was in the room…Oh, God, he wanted to be able to *SEE!*

Maureen O'Connell went to the kitchen of the small hospital and prepared some chicken soup for her patient. She was stirring the mixture when Dr. Anthony Martin walked in.

"Does he know?" she asked the physician.

"Not all of it," he replied. "I felt it better to only tell him what he needed to know. It's hard enough for him, right now."

"He's such a strong man. I think it's more difficult for them than it is for most humans."

"Yes. He's used to standing on his own two feet, Maureen."

"His friend is coming to see him. He'll notice the hospital, you know. He may realize…" She hesitated.

"Nicholas Stewart—a good man. He won't stand in our way, Maureen. He may be of some help to our Mr. Cabe."

Maureen took in a deep breath. She was relieved.

"Good," she nodded.

She turned off the heat from the stove. The soup was ready. She told the doctor goodnight, and started back to John Cabe's room.

Dr. Martin poured a cup of black coffee. He wondered if Nicholas Stewart would remember? It had been several months ago when the two had *met.* If he did remember, Dr. Martin would have some explaining to do, and it would involve *trusting Nicholas Stewart!*

Joseph finished bathing his patient. John still had the I.V. tubing to maintain, so the young man gave him a sponge bath and laid out fresh sheets and clothing.

"Tomorrow," Joseph told him, "they'll probably remove some of the tubes, so you can move around without all this restraint. You'll be able to move into the restroom and shower yourself, Mr. Cabe."

He helped John get into a clean hospital gown and changed the sheets on his bed.

John took a deep breath and leaned back on the cool pillow that Joseph gave him. He was glad he didn't have to explain things to him. Joseph didn't ask any questions, but he had a way of getting things done in a calm, orderly fashion. Joseph finished his job, just as Maureen entered with a tray.

"Good bath?" she asked.

"Very good," John replied, as he smelled the fresh, laundered bedding.

He was drained of all the anger that he felt earlier and he could smell the fragrance of the soup. It was the first thing since he awoke that seemed familiar to him. It smelled like home. He couldn't cook, but he could heat up a can of chicken soup. He thought about his home.

John's ranch had become his seclusion. He loved it there. When he first moved in, he had cleared the land and fixed up the main house by himself. The motion of riding a galloping horse over the hills nearby, gave him a peace he couldn't explain. He needed that peace between his flights for Transpower, his airline company.

John had lived in California for years, as Nick Stewart's private pilot, until Nick and Alexandra were married. He had been Nick's right-hand man and was also his oldest friend. When he saw Nick settle down with Alex, John felt something missing in his own life. He told Nick he wanted to try something new and when he saw the ad for Transpower, it seemed an answer to a prayer. He packed up the next month and moved to Arizona.

John Cabe settled into ranch life, like a stray adopting a family who feeds it. That was only a few months ago. Now, what would he do? The airline company was struggling, at best. When he purchased it, he knew it would take most of his energy to get it back on its feet.

"Here, Mr. Cabe."

The softness of his nurse's voice brought him back to reality. She rested the spoonful of soup barely on his lips, just below his nose. He took a deep breath, feeling the steam form moisture on his nostrils, and taking in the aroma. He took a sip. It was not only warm; it tasted very good to him.

"That tastes wonderful," he told Maureen.

"That's good to hear. Patients usually don't like hospital food. I find it's very tasty. I eat most of my meals here anyway."

"You do?"

"Yes. I'm a Special Duty nurse. I only have one or two patients at a time—those who may need a little something more..."

"Like me?" he interrupted.

She was afraid she might have offended him, but he took another sip of the hot liquid and, for the first time, she saw him smile.

"Like you," she answered.

John liked the sound of her voice. It had a slight lilt to it. He bet she was Irish-American. He asked her, and heard the surprise in her voice

"How did you know that?" she asked.

"Your voice still has an accent. I like it, Maureen."

When he said her name, it rolled off of his lips like honey. He asked her what her last name was.

She laughed, "That would have been a dead giveaway. It's McConnell."

"Oh, a good old Irish name—I knew it!"

Maureen McConnell wiped his mouth with a napkin and set the bowl on a table near his bed. She handed him a glass of juice, letting him find it, and then allowing him to hold it by himself.

John drank all of the sweet tasting juice and lifted the glass back into the air, where he thought she was still waiting. A small hand took the glass from him and he caught it before she had a chance to leave the room.

He was trembling.

"Please don't go, Maureen. It's so dark—and it's so lonely."

She knew he was frightened, despite how well he seemed to be doing today. She pulled over a chair, next to his bed, and held onto his hand.

"I'm not going anywhere, Mr. Cabe. I told you I'd be here when you need me. I'll sit right here."

John relaxed a little. He liked hearing her voice and feeling her closeness. He finally asked her about the woman whose life he had saved. It had been costly to him…too costly!

"How is the woman…the one in the car crash? What's her name anyway?"

Maureen McConnell smiled. This was a good sign. He was asking about someone else. She squeezed his hand and gave him a cool washcloth. John noticed he didn't have to ask Maureen for anything. She just took care of it.

"Her name is Katherine—Katherine B. Walcott," Maureen answered. "She likes to be called 'Kate'. She was burned badly on one side of her face and on her shoulder and arm. She had a lot of contusions, too—a lot of pain—but we think she'll make it. That's what we've all been praying for."

"What was she thinking of, driving that fast?"

John believed the woman should have known that she was endangering herself and everyone in her path. At this point, he had little sympathy for Kate Walcott!

"She was trying to kill herself, Mr. Cabe."

Maureen watched John Cabe's expression change.

"What? What did you say?"

"She didn't want to live, Mr. Cabe. She was trying to kill herself. She came pretty close to doing just that—if *you* hadn't been there."

Her answer was stopped short in mid-air by John's next question.

"Do you mean that I'm in this hospital bed, blinded, because this woman was *selfish* enough to try and take her own life?"

Maureen watched him, as he struggled with this truth.

It's going to get harder for him before it gets better.

She said a silent prayer for him and for Katherine Walcott, too. Maureen knew that he didn't know *why* Kate had tried such a desperate measure. He would know soon and, she wondered what his reaction would be to that news—when he found out.

"I should have let her die," he whispered under his breath.

"What?"

Maureen heard what he said. She was slightly disappointed at his reaction, but she understood it.

"You don't mean that, Mr. Cabe. You couldn't have done that, anyway. You aren't the kind of person to let an innocent woman burn to death."

John felt torn. He didn't want Maureen to hear him. She must have ears like his cat!

'Old Yeller' was John's adopted cat. He had come to the ranch one day and stayed, even though John Cabe didn't like cats that much. The raggedy feline had no tail at all, looked like a rabbit when he half-walked, half-hopped. He had ears that picked up noises no one around the ranch could hear—no one, but Old Yeller. It had saved his life more than once. He could hear a wild animal before it got close enough to harm him.

John wondered how the cat would be getting along, with him being laid up in a hospital. He'd ask Nick to go and check out the ranch tomorrow. He doubted if any of his ranch hands even missed him. Old Yeller could get water, at least and he was sure there were enough field mice to keep him alive, but the cat had gotten used to John being there—and vice-versa. John knew he was hooked when he put food out on the front porch, along with a bowl of milk. After that, the cat slept in his rocker everyday.

"I'm sorry I said that, Maureen—about letting her die. I didn't mean it."

John picked up on the disappointment in her voice.

Maureen watched him. It was so difficult for him. She wanted to comfort him, but she accepted his apology instead, and fluffed his pillow. She puttered around the room, picking up and straightening. John could hear the swish of her skirt, as she moved.

"What do you look like, Maureen?" he suddenly asked.

She was taken back by his question.

"What do *you think* I look like, Mr. Cabe?"

"Call me John, please. I guess we're stuck with each other for awhile. I mean—you're stuck with me! I'd *guess* that you're about five feet four inches tall, with red hair and green eyes—that's just because you're Irish."

She laughed at him, and found she couldn't stay angry.

"I have to be a red-head, huh? –*'just'* because I'm Irish?"

"Well, how close was I?"

"I'm five feet *five* inches, not four."

"And, the rest?"

He heard her sigh.

"Pretty much right on, John."

Saying his first name sounded almost too personal to her. She remembered some pleasant feelings from a long, long time ago.

"I knew it!" he boomed.

"It's time for your meds, John."

She was purposely changing the subject, and John knew he would have to let it go, for now. He was too tired anyway to try and flirt with his nurse. Maureen gave him his medicine and he washed it down with water.

"Will you stay until I drift off, Maureen?"

"Of course, John. Try and sleep. It's one of the best things you can do. Oh, by the way, your friend, Nicholas Stewart phoned. He said he would be here early in the morning. He said to let you know that he's bringing another friend with him, a Mr. Mac Timmons."

John paused. He didn't know what he would say to his friends. He first thought it would be easy to talk to them but now, he realized that it would be one of the most difficult days of his life.

Maureen held his hand as he tried to sleep. The meds were making him drowsy.

Chapter Three

Nick Stewart and his friend, Mac Timmons, flew into Clarksville and landed their helicopter near the Clarksville airport. Nick told Mac that he wanted to speak to John's doctor as soon as possible. He had to be sure what kind of care John was receiving. John had mentioned to Nick about *ruling out* a possible brain injury.

My God, that could mean anything from seizures to...

He didn't want to think about that. John was awake—that was good—and he was lucid and making sense. He was also blind!

Nick thought about John, who had helped save all of their lives just a few months ago—Nick's life, as well as Alexandra's and Mac's. Of all the people in the world, why John? He was certain his friend was asking the same questions.

Nicholas Stewart knew that he had to remain calm. He would have to dig deep into his newly found faith—that God knew what was going on, and it would turn out for good, as He promised.

He motioned to Mac and they ran from the copter, over to a waiting limo.

"Saint's Hospital, please," said Nick.

"Where?" the driver asked.

Nick pulled out a scribbled piece of notepaper and gave the driver the address that John had given him over the phone.

"Oh, *that* place. I'll have you there in just a few minutes."

The limo pulled out of the airport and onto the highway.

Nick wondered what he meant by the remark. Surely the sheriff's office wouldn't have taken John to a hospital that was less than adequate. He would get his friend moved immediately, if that were the case.

Within approximately five minutes, the limo driver pulled up to a small, contemporary, two-story building. The grounds were neat and well groomed. Nick and Mac got out of the limo and stepped into the drive-through near the front doors. When they entered the hospital, a young woman glanced up from the reception desk.

"Hello, may I help you?" she smiled.

"Yes, I'm Nicholas Stewart and this is Mr. Mac Timmons. We're here to see a friend, John Cabe. He's in Room 106."

"Mr. Stewart, of course—and Mr. Timmons. Please, come this way. Dr. Martin's been expecting you. He'd like to see you before you go in to speak with Mr. Cabe."

Nick noticed that the receptionist, although she appeared young, knew who they were and recognized John's name. She seemed to be efficient and didn't keep them waiting. The hospital, he also noticed, was spotless. There were highly waxed floors. The walls were a soft blue, freshly painted. There were some fine paintings hanging on the walls, too. Some prominent artists that he recognized had painted some of the canvasses. They didn't look like copies, either. As Nick looked more closely at one of them, he saw it was an original and figured the rest might be too!

"These must have cost this place a mint," he said to Mac.

There were of course, many pictures of Saints—Saint Paul, Saint Francis—and along the wall by the Chapel were many paintings of children and of angels. Nick Stewart found he was fascinated with a picture that the artist called, *Kingdom At Peace*. He had a copy of another painting that was similar, one by artist Edward Hicks, called *The Peaceable Kingdom*. It was one of his favorites and hung in his study at his home.

This one differed from any Nick had ever seen. He wondered who had painted it. The lion, lamb and oxen in the picture were similar to the one he owned, but this painting centered on a child, a boy, standing alone in the middle of the painting. Above was an angel standing watch.

It was the face of the angel that intrigued Nick. She was a young female with auburn hair. The light behind made her reddish strands glisten with gold and, her face was beautiful. He looked at the plate near the center of the frame. The title was: *Saint Bridget, Patron Saint of Ireland, protector of Children and Animals.* Nick tried to find an artist's name on the canvass, but it bore no name at all.

The receptionist finally reached the offices of Dr. Anthony Martin. She knocked softly on the door.

"Come in," a voice answered...a voice that sounded *familiar* to Nicholas Stewart.

Dr. Anthony Martin was getting up from behind his desk and heading to the door, when Mac Timmons and Nick Stewart entered.

"Mr. Stewart—Mr. Timmons," he nodded, and extended his hand. "It's so good to see you here. I thought we needed to get together before you see Mr. Cabe. I'd like to go over his condition with both of you, if that's all right?"

"Yes, we had the same thought," Nick answered, shaking the physician's hand.

Nick paused for a moment, as he looked directly into Anthony Martin's eyes.

"Dr. Martin, have we met before?"

Nick knew he had either seen or spoken with this tall, brown-haired man. Dr. Anthony Martin had features one wouldn't forget easily—strong jaw, eyes that pierced right through a person, and a smile that put you immediately at ease. The doctor commanded your attention, but he had a calmness that Nick would have desired in some of his own situations.

Nick glanced over at Mac to watch his reaction. Mac smiled at the doctor and shook his hand. The older man was a father figure to both Nicholas and to John. Mac treated them as he would his own sons. They had been through a lot together. Now, Dr. Anthony Martin was dealing with John Cabe's family, and he knew it.

Dr. Martin smiled. He neither lied nor offered the truth to

Nicholas.

"We may have met, Mr. Stewart. I do know some things about you." He smiled and continued.

"I've read every news article about how you and your friends saved the United States and other countries from the destruction of a terrorist plot. I think I owe you a *Thank you,* Mr. Stewart—Mr. Timmons—as others do."

Nick was barely listening as he continued to wonder where he had seen this person before. Dr. Martin was obviously avoiding telling him. He was so familiar…it was at the edge of his mind. Then, Nick returned to his questions about John.

"You don't owe me anything," he replied. "Anyone would have done the same thing. Getting back to John—tell us what happened. How is he getting along?"

"Mr. Cabe pulled a woman from a burning car, as you may know, and the car exploded. A heavy piece of metal hit him in the head. Another glass fragment was found embedded under the skin, and very close to his right eye.

"His blindness, which is in both eyes, may have been caused by both traumas, or, it could be emotional. I just don't know, until we run more tests. He's had a CT Scan, but I want an MRI run, along with some other tests. Mr. Cabe is frightened, Mr. Stewart. This is difficult for him, as you can imagine."

"You said there was a fire. The woman was burned. Was John burned too?"

"The woman was pretty badly burned on her face and shoulder. Mr. Cabe had only minor burns on one hand. He attempted to put out the fire on her clothing.

"He also had several cuts and contusions. His face, when he was brought in, looked like a porcupine! There were bits of glass stuck everywhere! They had to be removed in surgery.

"He hasn't had a seizure, and he seems to know what's going on around him, which is very good, especially after not waking up for almost six days. We thought he was drifting into a deep coma, but he seemed to be alert when he woke up.

"I've assigned a Special Duty nurse, Maureen McConnell, to stay with him twelve hours a day. Our male nurse, Joseph, is with him most of the night. He's getting a lot of attention. As you can tell, we're a small hospital, but we're specifically made for trauma patients…and we have a burn unit too."

"Dr. Martin, anything you need, I have the money to provide."

"Thank you, Mr. Stewart. That's very generous. When you see our facilities, I think you'll understand. We seem to have everything we need. I'll take you to see Mr. Cabe now. Later, we can schedule that tour—whenever you'd like."

When Nick and Mac entered John's room, they weren't sure how he would react to them.

"Hey, buddy," Nick said as he went over to the bed to hug his friend.

He wasn't surprised that John clung to him longer than usual. John smiled, but couldn't speak. He was clearly overwhelmed by the circumstances. Mac went over and took his hand.

"John, you old cowboy!"

Mac hadn't seen John since he moved to Clarksville and to his ranch.

"Mac! Nick—I've missed the two of you so much. You've got to see it, Mac—my ranch. You won't believe it. Nick, I can't wait till you go out there."

John stopped, unsure of what more to say. Then, he almost whispered to them.

"Pretty fine mess that I've gotten myself into this time, isn't it?"

"We've had worse, John," said Nick, remembering their backgrounds. "You're going to come out of this one, too. Now, tell us. What can we do to help?"

It was good to have Nick and Mac here. John could ask them to do anything and they'd do it, no questions asked. Then, he thought of his ranch and asked Nick and Mac to go check on it, and to get in touch with his foreman, Kent Able, and find out what was going on. He went on to ask them to check on 'Old Yeller'.

"See about who?" Mac asked.

"He's my cat—don't laugh! He's about as tough as I am…as I was. He's a yellow Manx cat—no tail at all but a powder puff. I need someone to put down some food and water on the front porch for him."

John realized what they must have been thinking about him

owning a cat and he had to laugh.

"I know. I know what you're thinking, but we've become friends. Nick, he's been the only critter that doesn't gripe. He just listens to me. He may not trust you at first, but he'll get used to you. Would you do that for me? Would you see about the ranch and how my cat is getting along?"

"Of course, John. Now, about your help here in the hospital—may I get you a private nurse, a physical therapist, anything? Just tell me! I plan consulting with a doctor in Los Angeles to make sure you're getting the best of care. If we need to move you, we will. You know you can stay with Alexandra and me. You know that, John."

Nicholas Stewart wasn't certain what John's medical needs would be until he had Dr. Martin send the results of his tests to Nick's specialist in L.A., but he would move heaven and earth for John Cabe, if he had to.

"I seem to be getting pretty decent care, Nick. Have you seen my nurse, yet? She's Irish, you know? She's usually around—a redhead, five feet, five inches. She's here almost twenty-four seven!"

"That sounds like the old John," Mac whispered to Nick. "He always had an eye for the ladies."

But, he can't see her…how did he know all of that about this nurse named Maureen?

Both men thought the same thing at approximately the same time. Nick looked at Mac and shrugged.

"No, we didn't see her yet, John," he said.

"I have to tell you. I don't know how I'm going to make it, guys. I'm so angry! If I had just called for help on my car phone and waited when I saw that wreck, I wouldn't be here now."

John Cabe's face changed, as he thought of the accident. Nick saw the bitterness take hold of his friend.

"Did you know that the woman I pulled out of the wreck was trying to kill herself? Can you believe that? Nick, she didn't want to live, anyway. Why did I have to be the one to save her bloody…?"

Both Mac and Nicholas heard the frustration in John's voice. He was a hero, but he ended up a victim too. Nick pulled up a chair and sat down beside his bed.

"Have you talked to her yet, John?" he asked his friend.

"Are you kidding? I'm the last person she wants to see, and vice-versa."

"But, John, you need to talk to her. She will want to see you later. I'm certain of that. You better be prepared for what you're going to say to her. That's going to be hard, for certain. I heard that she's been badly burned. She may have some scarring."

Nick saw from the expression on John's face that he didn't want to think or talk about this now. He backed off and Mac motioned to Nick to get ready to leave. He, too, sensed this conversation had reached an end, for now.

"John? We're going to go out to your ranch right now. We'll take care of everything there and we'll be back as soon as we can. I'll bring you back some home-cooked food for lunch, too."

It became evident to both Nick and John that Mac was trying to help change the subject.

"Yeah," replied John. "That will be good. Thanks. I'll look forward to hearing what you think of my place—and my cat."

Although he sounded a little better, Mac knew John Cabe wasn't ready to face anything yet. He was still in shock. Mac gave John one of his famous bear hugs and said that he'd see him later in the afternoon.

Nick Stewart looked around John's room before he left. It was neat and clean. Someone had placed fresh flowers on his dresser. He had ice and water and he could make it until they returned. Nick stopped on the way out the door and touched the door, saying a prayer for his friend and one for the woman whose life John had saved.

"We'll be back, John. Oh, by the way, Alexandra sends her love. She told me to tell you that she would have come with Mac and me, but she had to care for Sabrina. When I left them, Sabrina had a cold and had claimed Alex's bed for her own. Sabrina said to tell her Uncle John 'hello' for her too. She's grown a foot since you've seen her, John. I imagine when our child's well, Alex will be on her way here."

"That beautiful wife and daughter of yours, Nick—they're the best. I'd love to be able to see them—really see them. Still, feeling them, talking to them, that's what I'll settle for right now."

Mac and Nick went into the hallway of the hospital, where they ran into Dr. Martin. Nick told the physician that they would be back this afternoon and he asked if they could bring John back some food.

"What about his diet?"

"John can probably eat a normal diet and I don't think it will hurt him if he feels like it. His body will tell him what he can and can't have right now...but, having you here with him will mean more to him than food or medicine."

Nick asked Dr. Martin if he could access John's records, in order to send them off to a specialist for a second opinion. He wondered if the doctor might object.

"Certainly. I'll have my secretary get the records ready. And, Mr. Stewart, I'll be happy to give you that tour, whenever you want. I'm very proud of my staff. They care for the whole human being here at Saint's. No one is a number, I can assure you."

The way Anthony Martin said it, with total openness, made Nick feel more comfortable. Nick Stewart still could not remember where he had met this doctor before, but he knew it would come to him.

Chapter Four

John was wondering where Maureen was. She was usually at his bedside earlier than this. He wanted her to meet Nick and Mac. It was good to know they would take care of details regarding his ranch and they would make sure the cat was okay.

"Stupid animal," but John kept thinking about Yeller.

It was all he had left now. It was the cat that he talked to, the cat that he held, and it was the cat that kept him company.

"Get a life, J.C.," he muttered

"I'm trying," he answered.

"This is really bad. Now, I'm talking to myself. Heck, I'm having a whole conversation."

John pressed the buzzer for the nurse. He needed to talk to another human!

A few minutes later, Maureen came into his room. She told him who she was, as she always did when she entered. It wasn't necessary anymore. John could sense who it was. He could smell her cologne and hear the swish of her uniform, hear the lightness of her walk on the tile floors.

"Maureen, I was wondering where you were hiding. I wanted you to meet my friends. They just left a few minutes ago. I bragged on my pretty nurse to them."

"I'm sorry, Mr. Cabe. I was tied up with another patient."

John thought, after what she had told him, that he was her only patient. She stayed with him for such long periods of time; he didn't see how she would have time left for anyone else.

"Maureen, I thought you were going to call me 'John'."

"Are you sure that's all right with you?"

"All right? I don't have anyone that calls me Mr. Cabe. You're the first. Dr. Martin is the second—I don't even know who 'Mr. Cabe' is. I never really knew him."

Maureen chuckled.

"All right. I get it. 'John' it is!"

Maureen McConnell fluffed his pillow and changed the water in the vase of flowers. She brought him some fresh ice water and then sat down beside him.

"What can I do for you, John?"

He hated to tell her that he only wanted her company, when she had other patients who might need her.

"How is she today?"

"How is who?"

"You know. Kate...Katherine Walcott?"

"Oh, I'm not sure, John. I haven't seen Kate this morning. Dr. Martin's taking care of her burns. Would you like to go and see her? I can get a wheelchair for you and take you to her room. We can check on her together."

"No!"

He raised his voice, almost shouting at Maureen. He heard the harshness in his own voice, took in a deep breath, and paused.

"I mean...I can't do that now. I just can't—not yet."

"It's all right John. I'll try and find out how she's doing—see what's going on, but you're going to have to face her sooner or later. Her car insurance company wants to talk to you, too. They're not about to pay anything in a case of attempted suicide."

"I hope not! Let me know how she is, will you? But, don't go out of your way. Who is your other patient—the one you were with earlier?"

CLYDENE R. BRANDT

He was curious and a little jealous. He didn't know why.

"It's a child—a little boy. He was brought in this morning. He wasn't expected to make it this long, but he's managed to hold on. He was in an auto accident."

"My God, that's so sad," said John. "It's not fair, is it?"

"It may not seem that way, to us."

"Why would God let a child be hurt?"

"If you had those answers, John, would it help you find some peace—peace about your own accident?"

She had hit a nerve. His faith was shaken to the core. He had no answers. Everything that he believed once, lay in shattered pieces, all around him. His fait. He had no faith left, except in his friends and himself.

He answered her, "I don't think I'll ever find peace again, Maureen."

"That's not true, John. I will promise you that. Will you believe me? You will find peace, again—and love, more than you *ever dreamed possible.*"

Her voice was full of a passion that he hadn't heard before. It would have been impossible *not* to believe her. When she touched his hand, warmth went through him that he hadn't felt in awhile, and he smiled and caught her other hand.

"I have to believe you, Maureen. You've never lied to me. Promise me that you never will."

Maureen trembled. He didn't know everything yet—and she knew that, but she was determined not to lie to him, even when he found out the truth.

"I promise. I will never lie to you, John."

John wanted to feel her face. He wanted to try and see what she looked like. He wasn't sure why it was important. She'd think he was crazy to ask her that, at least this fast. He thought of her warmth toward him.

She has a good soul. She really cares about her patients.

John Cabe spoke softly, "The child, Maureen—the little boy they brought in. Go back to him now. I can wait. He needs you more than I do."

Maureen smiled, an unselfish act—he is getting better!

"If you're certain John—I'll just be about thirty minutes. Joseph is on duty now. If you need anything, he will be right here."

She handed him the call button.

"I'll be fine. You go and take care of that child."

He could hear the swish of her skirt, as she left his room. John was curious about the hospital and, he was curious about his own perseverance. He needed to get up from the bed and move around the room. He wanted to feel everything and see where things were placed — see if he could walk around without bumping into anything. He put his feet down on the floor. It felt cool. It was tile, as he suspected. He ran his feet to one side and then the other, seeing if he could find his slippers.

"Aha! Right where Joseph must have left them, barely under my bed."

He slipped his feet into the soft leather shoes and rose to his feet. He was still weak and he held onto the side of the bed to steady himself. John Cabe decided that he would make his way around the bed and then go further, each time making a larger and larger circle, until he had covered every inch of the room.

As he edged around the bed, he found that his chart was hanging on the foot of the bed. On the other side, he ran into the I.V. stand and caught it before it fell over. He was disconnected from any tubes presently, but someone had left it in the room.

John reached down and rubbed the sheets with his fingertips. He moved to the head of the bed. There was a nightstand on this side. He ran his hand along the top of it. Phone — box of tissues — vase with flowers. He leaned down to smell them, and he had the need to touch them. There were roses, zinnias — was this a daisy? He made it from one side of the bed to the other and started back.

When he got around from where he began, John fell back into the bed, exhausted. He didn't know why he was so tired, but he felt as if he had accomplished something. He took a deep breath. His head was still hurting. If he could rest a few minutes, he would start again. He closed his eyes.

Mac and Nick found John's foreman, Kent Able, and told him what had happened to John. The sheriff had been out the next day and had let Kent know John was in an accident, but didn't have much information at that time.

"I've meant to go see him, but we've really been busy here. I figured he'd rather have me taking care of the ranch."

Nick gave him John's instructions of what to do next, and then he and Mac walked up to the house.

The ranch house was small, but looked as if John had put a lot of work into the place. It was evident to Nick, as he walked up the steps to the front porch, that John must love the place. There was a hand-carved swing that he had made and hung. There was also a rocker to match—and, on the rocker, was a scraggly yellow-striped cat. The cat looked up and yawned, as Nick and Mac came up the steps.

"There he is," said Nick.

"Hey there, old fellow—your pop's pretty worried about you."

The cat stared at Nick, then jumped down, twisting and turning through his legs.

"Well, he's pretty friendly," said Mac.

"He's hungry. Let's go inside. We can find his food."

The cat ran ahead of Nick and when he opened the front door, the cat ran inside, jumping up on the island between the living room and the kitchen.

"He must know where it's kept. Animals—they're all a lot smarter than humans sometime," said Mac.

Nick found the cat food and put some into a dish, then put the dish down on the floor and watched, as the cat ate eagerly. Old Yeller was purring and eating at the same time, glad that a human *finally* had come back to feed him.

Nick got a bowl of water and placed it beside the food.

"Wish all problems were solved that easy," he said to Mac.

"Now, we need to find John's mail. We can bring it with us when we go back to the hospital. I'll read it to him and mail off any bills that are due. I wonder if the men have been paid? Guess I'll have to ask John's foreman. I can pay them, if need be."

Nick Stewart was used to taking charge. He always took care of details and it was one of his strengths that Mac admired. Mac or John would have done anything Nick asked, but now, it was John's turn and Nick would do the same for him.

"What can I do to help, Nick?"

"Mac, I want you to see if John has any neighbors that he's close to, and if there are, they need to be told about his situation. He may need help, when he gets home. Also, there may be someone that will come over and feed the cat. If not, I'll have his foreman do it."

Mac was on the way out the door to find out about John's neighbors. Nick and the cat were left alone.

"Well, Old Yeller—what a name! I guess you and I can see if anything needs to be done here. John wasn't the best housekeeper in the world as I remember, but this place doesn't look too bad. We'll straighten up, but we can't move anything. He needs to remember where everything is when he gets home."

The cat sat on the divider and appeared to be listening to everything that Nick Stewart said.

Nick washed the few dishes in the sink, poured out the old coffee and washed the pot. Then, he went to the door and walked down the path to the mailbox. He picked up all of the mail and walked back to the ranch house.

The cat had settled on the rocking chair again, washing himself. Nick sat down on the swing and sorted through John's mail.

"I need to phone Alexandra, Yeller," he said. "She'll be worried about John."

"Good grief! Now, I'm talking to the cat!"

He took his cell phone from his shirt pocket and dialed his wife.

When Maureen came back into John Cabe's hospital room, she found him asleep and on top of the covers. He looked peaceful.

"Looks can be deceiving, Maureen."

Dr. Martin had slipped in behind her. It was as if he had read her thoughts.

"I know. He's a man full of turmoil. It's good to see him rest a minute, though."

"Kate Walcott just asked to see him, Maureen."

"What? I didn't think she was well enough..."

"She's insisting. I don't know how Mr. Cabe feels, but for her sake, he needs to be brought down to her room as soon as he's awake."

"He won't like that, you know?"

Maureen thought about the earlier battle that she had encountered on this subject. John Cabe wasn't ready.

"I know. I believe it's necessary. You'll arrange it?"

"Yes."

Maureen knew what she had to do. She woke John up, softly brushing his hair back, with her hand.

"What—who—who is it?"

"It's me John. It's Maureen. You fell asleep. Do you want to get under the covers?"

"Oh, Maureen, no, no. I got up, went the long distance of around the bed and back. I guess I fell asleep. I'm going to see the rest of this room or die trying. Maureen, could you help me? Guide me around? I want to be able to visualize what it looks like."

"Of course, that's a wonderful idea. I'll help you. We can start right now, if you want."

"I do. When Nick and Mac get back, I want to be able to get up and at least find a chair."

Maureen helped him back up. She would have to bring up the subject of seeing Katherine Walcott soon and she prayed for the right words.

"John? You remember when I asked before—about your seeing Kate Walcott?"

"Yes. I remember," he answered.

He knew she was leading up to something.

"Well, she's very ill, but she's asking to speak with you. I think you should go and see her."

She could feel the muscles in his arm tense.

"I don't know if I can do that, Maureen."

He didn't want to talk to this woman. He hated what she had cost him. Maureen had no right to make him feel guilty about this!

"John if I didn't think that it would help you, I wouldn't ask. Do you remember when I promised that I would always tell you the truth?"

"Yes, of course."

"The truth is that you will always feel bad until you talk to her. Please…"

It wasn't what he expected her to say, but something in the tone of her voice made him believe every word she was saying. He found himself agreeing to go and talk to Katherine Walcott.

Maureen helped John walk around his room. She showed him where everything was. He found his toilet articles and the clean sheets and then Maureen showed him where the closet was and the light switch. Later, she found his robe and got him into a wheelchair. It was then that she asked if he was ready?

"I guess it's now or never," he answered.

Maureen wheeled him down the hall—to Katherine Walcott's room...

As Maureen and John entered Katherine's room, John smelled a strong medicinal odor and remembered that Katherine had been badly burned and was being treated daily with baths and changes of bandages. He and Maureen had to wear a mask to be in the room with her for now. John cringed at the thought of the pain that she must be going through.

"Katherine?" whispered Maureen, "Mr. Cabe's here. He's come to see you, just as you asked."

John leaned forward. He could hear her breathing and he could hear the strain in each breath that she took.

"Miss Walcott? I'm John Cabe. What is it that you wanted?"

He heard a voice that was almost a whisper.

"Mr. Cabe? I had to see you. I'm so sorry. Please say you forgive me. I'm so sorry about what happened to you."

John didn't know how to reply. He hadn't expected this. She sounded so weak and he wondered if she were really going to make it through this.

"Miss Walcott, don't worry about anything right now. You just get well. Try and rest. We can talk later, when we're both feeling better, okay?"

John didn't expect to be civil with her, let alone, feel sorry for her. He was squirming in his wheelchair and just wanted to get out of there and back to his own room.

"Maureen?" he asked.

"Yes, John, I'm right here."

"Shouldn't we go and let Miss Walcott rest?"

It was a plea for help and Maureen knew it. She didn't answer him.

"No, wait," Katherine Walcott interrupted. "I have to tell you something—I have to tell you—please, don't go yet."

"Calm down, Miss Walcott," John replied. "We're still here. What is it that you have to tell me? I'll stay a minute more, but you *have to rest!*"

"Thank you. I wanted to tell you why I was driving that fast. This is so difficult...I...I was trying to kill myself, Mr. Cabe. I'm so sorry. It was my entire fault—your accident. God, I may never forgive myself. I vow that I will, in some way, repay you. I will never rest until I can do that!"

What's she going to do...miraculously restore my eyesight?

John bit his tongue to keep from saying what he was thinking. Instead, he motioned to Maureen to leave.

"That's not necessary, Miss Walcott. I'm sorry, but I have to leave. I hope you feel better."

He had to get away from this young woman—out of here! He felt like he couldn't breathe. Maureen sensed his reaction and told Katherine that she would return a little later. She pushed John back to his room. She saw his clenched fists and knew he was upset.

"How did that help, Maureen? How in the world did that help either of us?"

He was angry and frustrated with Kate Walcott, and with himself. He was even angry with Maureen.

Chapter Five

Nick and Mac ate dinner at the local diner in Clarksville and then picked up a 'Blue Plate Special' to go. The food was pretty good for a *Mom and Pop* business. Mac thought John would enjoy eating something besides hospital fare for one night.

On the drive back from the ranch, Mac mentioned to Nick that he found a couple who lived down the road from John who would come over, feed the cat, and pick up his mail, until he returned home.

"They seem real nice," said Mac. "They're retired and their last name is Simpson."

"Good. At least that's one worry John won't have to think about."

"Did you talk to Alexandra yet?" asked Mac.

"I did. She's ready to fly out here in a few days. She can cheer John up, I know."

Nick remembered when he first introduced John to Alex. They were *immediate* friends. Later, they had become *best friends.* He smiled. If things had been different, John would probably have dated Alexandra, but, Nick and Alex had fallen in love—in fact, it was love at first sight...something he would never have believed in before

Alexandra. He still felt that way. She was his soul mate and he missed her. He missed Sabrina too. He'd be happy to see his wife and child again, even though he had only been gone one day.

"I'm going to go on that tour as soon as we get back to the hospital, Mac, while you take John his dinner. I'll be along as soon as I speak to Doctor Martin again."

"He seems like a nice person, Nick. I get the feeling he really cares about John."

"There's something familiar about him, Mac. I know I've met him before. I just can't remember where."

"Maybe he's just got a familiar face, like he says, Nick. He really puts people at ease, doesn't he?"

Nicholas Stewart didn't answer. It was something important—he had to remember!

They arrived at the hospital and Nick headed straight for Dr. Anthony Martin's office while Mac went to John's room.

When Mac entered, John was sitting up on the edge of the bed. A young man was helping him try to stand and walk to his chair. Mac smiled and introduced himself. The young man nodded.

"How are you feeling, John?"

"Oh, I'm feeling better, Mac. So, how's the ranch? Everything still there?"

"Everything was fine. We found your cat and Nick fed him. Then, we found some neighbors who said they'd take care of him while you're in the hospital. They're going to pick up your mail, too."

"Who?"

"An older couple—live just down the road from you—the Simpsons. Do you know them?"

John hated to tell Mac that he still hadn't met any of his neighbors. He had been too busy with the business and the ranch.

"I haven't met them. I'm sure they're okay if you say they are. Are they retired?"

"That's what they tell me—they seem real nice. You should go and meet them when you can. They were pretty worried about you and told me to tell you not to concern yourself with anything. They'll do anything they can to help."

"How's the cat?"

"He was asleep in the rocker when we left. He was pretty friendly to us. Nick said that was because he was hungry. I think he actually liked us," Mac grinned.

"If he didn't, he wouldn't have had anything to do with you, hungry or not. He's a doggone good judge of character, unlike some humans," John laughed.

Joseph asked John if he wanted to try another walk around the room, or just sit in the chair. John chose the chair. He wanted to talk to Mac alone. When Joseph asked if he could leave, John thanked him and told him he could. Then, John turned to Mac.

"Where's Nick?" he asked.

"Gone to take a tour of the hospital. He wants to make sure that you have the best care. You know Nick, John. He won't rest until he knows that."

John thought of his friend. Nick was like that. He knew that any of the three friends would do anything for the other, even give up their life for the other, if it came to that. He thought about how lucky he was to have them.

"Mac, if I don't regain my sight..." John began.

"Don't say that. Don't even think that. You'll see again, John. I feel it *here.* Mac took John's hand and laid it over his heart.

"I just meant—if I don't—even for a little while—I have to train myself to function—I have to be able to take care of myself, Mac. That's what I'm thinking about. How do I begin?"

Mac heard the emotion in John's voice. He wondered if John was planning something, and Mac had a grave concern about what that would be.

"John? You wouldn't do anything—foolish, would you?"

"Good grief, no! I wouldn't try and do away with myself, if that's what you're asking. I just need a plan. I need to know what the doctor is thinking and how I'm going to cope with whatever he tells me. I can't see, Mac and I have to know how to make it, if my sight doesn't return—even if it's temporary."

Mac knew John Cabe wouldn't rest, until he knew he could live his life—with or *without his sight.*

"You know Nick and I will help you, anyway we can. If it's therapists, or teachers, or whatever you need, we'll be there with you, John."

"That's all I could ask for Mac. Thank you."

He was moved by what the old man said to him and John believed him. He just needed to hear Mac say it.

Nick Stewart found Dr. Martin in his office. The physician was looking at some x-rays.

"Mr. Stewart! Good to see you again. I just got some of Mr. Cabe's test results back. I must say, they're about what I expected."

"Oh, what's that, Dr. Martin?"

"Mr. Cabe's blindness appears to be caused by something more emotional than physical. There's no physical reason that he shouldn't be seeing."

"Are you saying his blindness is psychological?"

"Not so easily diagnosed, I'm afraid. I do believe that he's blocking out something. I don't know what it is. His blindness is real. That makes it doubly hard. He needs to talk to someone like a counselor, or someone he trusts—someone who can find out what's at the heart of this. Knowing Mr. Cabe, he probably won't accept that as the answer he wants to hear."

"You're certain, Dr. Martin ?"

"As certain as anyone can be. You're welcome to send the test results to any doctor that you trust."

Nick wasn't sure that was necessary anymore. He had begun to trust this man. He told Dr. Martin that he'd think over what to do and mentioned that he would like that tour of the hospital now, if the doctor had time.

Dr. Martin seemed glad to get out of his office. He opened the door for Nick and began the tour.

"We'll begin in the children's wing, if that's all right with you," he said, as he led the way.

Nick walked behind Dr. Martin, as he opened the doors to the children's wing. If he had expected a dismal unit, he didn't get it. There were drawings on the walls, balloons on some of the beds, and a toy corner, filled with educational toys, books and physical therapy equipment—expensive equipment.

The walls were light blue, but someone had painted a large tree on one of the walls and the leaves were handprints, with the name of a child painted on each one. Dr. Martin and Nick walked over to a young boy, who was in the first bed.

"Hello, son," Nick said, "How are you feeling?"

"Hi, sir," the child beamed when he saw Nick. "I'm getting a lot better. My name's Matthew. What's yours?"

"I'm Nick Stewart, son."

No one had asked Nicholas Stewart his name in a long, long time. It was refreshing. This child had never heard of him.

"Hi, Nick. I was going to try and put this model airplane together. Want to help me?"

"Sure, Matthew. Did your parents give you this?"

Nick knew immediately that he had said the wrong thing from the way the boy's face clouded over. He glanced back at Dr. Martin.

"Maureen, our nurse, gave Matthew the plane. She knows he likes planes, right Matthew? Tell Mr. Stewart about Maureen, Matthew."

As Nick looked at the doctor and then back at the boy, he realized the physician had changed the subject—away from the boy's parents, to the nurse that John had mentioned. Nick suspected something terrible must have happened to the boy's parents.

"Miss Maureen bought it for me. She's really nice."

Matthew handed the box to Nick.

"Well, now, we'll have to look at these instructions, Matthew. Dr. Martin, I may be awhile. Can I have a rain check on our tour? Matthew and I have a plane to put together."

Dr. Martin smiled. Nick Stewart caught on quickly. He was happy to delay the tour for a child—anytime. He told Nick he'd return in about half an hour and he backed away and watched them for a minute. He would tell Nick later about the boy's parents.

Anthony Martin had set up this introduction. Nick Stewart was a good man—a father, before he was a celebrity—a husband, before he was a star—and, a friend, before he was a hero. He and Matthew were going to get along fine, and then he'd introduce the child to the person who would change his life forever, *John Cabe!*

Mac watched John eat the last of his 'blue plate special'.

"Mmm, that's about the best piece of pie I've tasted in a long time, Mac."

Mac watched him scrape the last bit of apple pie from the plate.

"Thought you'd like the food. Nick and I ate dinner there. It's a pretty fair little diner."

"I'm afraid I haven't had much time to come into town, Mac. The airline has gobbled up all of my time, lately."

"How about your money? Has it taken a lot of that, too?"

John lowered his head. Mac knew how to cut right through the fluff and get to the point, all right.

"It's taken most of my savings just getting the airline back in shape. This was the first month that we were going to be able to make our payroll and actually show a profit."

"You're wondering what you're going to do now, right?"

"Pretty much."

"You know you don't have to worry, kid. I've saved a lot of money. What else am I going to do with it? What you need for your airline is another *partner...me!*"

"Mac—I don't' know what to say—I..."

John fought to find the words that his heart felt.

"Just say yes, John. That's all you have to say."

"Yes, Mac. Thank you. I promise I'll pay you back. I promise we'll make the money back."

"Good. So, now I have a partnership in an airline. For a "chauffeur" of Nick Stewart, that's not bad!"

Mac had to laugh. He knew he was more than Nick's driver. Nick and John were like the boys he never had and he loved them both. Now, John had a problem—at last he could help.

"Mac, I'll let Nick look over the books. He can advise what we need to do. I guess the first thing is to look for a pilot. I have to have someone who will take my place for awhile, until I know something."

"Don't worry. I know you and Nick will take care of the details. Meantime, why don't I go to the newspaper and run an ad for a pilot. That's something I can do to make myself useful. I'll call Alexandra and see how I should word the ad. That's her expertise."

John thought Alex Stewart. "I miss her, Mac. How is she doing?"

"She's fine—more in love than ever with Nick. You know Alexandra. She's kept busy with her old newspaper, sending in articles and such. She had some publishing house want her to write a story about Nick, but she turned it down. Right now, she's doing some freelance. Mostly, she's making a home for Nick and Sabrina. I don't think I've ever seen that little girl as happy, not since she lost her mother. Nicholas loves them both so much. I didn't think he would get over his first wife's death, but he's as content now as I've ever seen him."

"I'm glad. I'd love to visit with Sabrina and Alex. I hope they can come down here soon."

"I think she's planning a visit soon, John. She told Nick that as soon as Sabrina gets over her cold, she plans coming down. She may leave Sabrina with her nanny a few days—doesn't want that child to miss too much school, you know."

"Life has certainly changed for us, hasn't it Mac? Remember when it was just the three of us? You, Nick and me? We go back a long way."

At that moment, Nick Stewart entered the room. He had a small boy in a wheelchair with him.

"Hey guys, I want you to meet someone. John and Mac, this is Matthew."

"Hi," said Matthew.

"Well, hello there, young fellow. I'm Mac Timmons. It's nice to meet you."

"John, Matthew just put a model plane together. He wants to be a pilot when he grows up. I told him I knew the best pilot in the U.S. He wanted to meet you."

Nick pushed Matthew next to John's chair.

"Hello, Matthew," John said. He extended his hand and a small, chubby hand felt its way into it.

John grinned as he felt the child's hand.

"Hi, are you really blind?" the child asked.

"For the time being—guess it's going to be hard to fly a plane for awhile, huh, Matthew?"

"I guess so. I'm sorry you can't see. I was going to show you my model. Nick helped me put it together."

"So that's where you've been," said Mac, "We might have known you wouldn't make it past the children's wing."

Nick Stewart smiled at Mac and nodded.

"Go ahead and let John feel that model, Matthew. I bet he can tell you what kind of plane it is, even without seeing it."

John took the model airplane from the child, holding it carefully. He felt the wings, the body, and the tail.

"Good job, Matthew. I bet this is an old 'flying tiger'."

"Wow! How'd you know that?" the child asked.

"I told you he was good, Matthew. I bet if you'd ask, he could almost promise you a ride on his plane—when you both get out of here."

The child looked at Nick and then back at John.

"Would you, John? Would you, really?"

"Sure, kid. I may not be the one flying it, but you've got a promise."

"Wow! Thanks, John…Nick, thanks…wow!"

Nick Stewart and Mac were grinning like two Cheshire cats. It was the first time they saw John Cabe happy since they arrived.

"Okay, I think that's about enough excitement for today, Matthew. I promised Dr. Martin I'd only keep you a little while. I think we'd better head back to your bed."

"I'll be happy to transport him, Nick. You stay here and chat with John."

Mac took the back of Matthew's wheelchair and started for the door.

"Here we go young man. Say goodbye, for a while anyway. I have a feeling we're going to be seeing a lot more of you."

The child waved goodbye, as Mac pushed him back to the children's wing. Nick Stewart sat down, next to John. He wasn't sure if he should mention what Dr. Martin had told him yet, and then decided he should wait for Dr. Martin to tell John about his eyesight.

"Well, bud, how was dinner?"

Nick had noticed the empty containers near the bed.

"Best in town, I hear. It tasted good. Thanks."

John told Nick about his company and about Mac's offer to become a partner. He asked him if he would go over his books and tell Mac everything he needed to know before he invested any money.

"You know I'll be glad to do that. John, if you need money, you know I'll help"

"No, Nick. I mean, Mac is getting a partnership. I don't want charity. I want to do this thing on my own—it's not that I don't appreciate your offer—you've had to bail me out so often, please…"

Nick knew how John felt. His pride was a tough thing to get around. He would wait and he promised John that he would look over the books.

"I'll always be there for you, John. You know if you change your mind, I'll help in anyway I can. By the way, that cat of yours has made himself at home. Did Mac tell you?"

Nick Stewart thought changing the subject right now might be a very good idea.

"He did. He's a tough old feline, Nick. Reminds me of Mac," John laughed.

"Hey, where's that pretty nurse you told me about? I have yet to meet her."

"Maureen? I'm surprised you didn't find her in the children's wing. She told me she was spending time with a child there…a little boy…the child was pretty bad off, from what I heard. Hey, what's the story on Matthew?"

"I almost ruined that meeting, John. I asked him if his parents bought that model plane. Dr. Martin told me later that both of his parents had been killed in an auto accident. Poor kid! I thought he needed some cheering up. When he mentioned he liked planes, the first person I thought about was you. Could you keep a check on him while you're here? I know he needs someone to talk to."

"Sure, I'd be glad to. He's a nice kid. I bet Maureen knows him. I'll have her wheel me down there tomorrow to see him again."

"John? Did you see Kate Walcott, yet?"

"Yes, I did. It was hard, Nick. She's in a lot of pain. She asked to see me—wants me to forgive her—said she'd *make it up to me.* Isn't that a laugh?"

John wasn't smiling any longer. The thought of Katherine Walcott made him turn cold inside.

"I can't help think that you need to go and talk to her again, John. I know it's hard. Forgiveness is never easy, but sometimes it's necessary for your own healing."

Nick tried not to sound judgmental. He was thinking about what Dr. Martin told him—that John's blindness could be psychological. Kate Walcott might hold part of that healing in her hands.

"Now you sound like Maureen! I've never known anyone who could talk me into doing something I really didn't want to do. You need to meet her. You're two of a kind!"

John had to grin. He couldn't stay angry with Nick or Maureen.

"Well, I say I'm in good company then," said Nick.

He believed that John could have a crush on this nurse that he talked about so much.

"What do you say I press the 'call' button and bring her in here?" John asked.

"I've been waiting to meet this angel of mercy. Please, allow me…"

Nick took the call buzzer and rang for John's nurse. Yes, he wanted to meet this Maureen McConnell he had heard so much about from John and from Matthew.

Joseph saw the light above John's door and started for his room, when Dr. Martin stopped him. He motioned for Joseph to come with him.

"I think we need to let Maureen answer this call, Joseph."

"But, sir—they need…"

"It will be okay."

Maureen McConnell headed for John's room. As she entered, Nick Stewart felt his jaw drop. Standing in front of him was a nurse that John had described as having red hair, green eyes and stood five feet five. The woman didn't fit the description at all. She did have auburn hair and had an Irish accent when she said 'hello' to John. Other than that, she was petite, middle-aged, and hardly noticeable, except for her demeanor. She glowed with warmth. Maureen walked over to him and extended her hand.

"You must be Mr. Stewart," she smiled.

Nick was speechless. She was familiar—very familiar. Where? Where had they met? As he took her hand, a feeling of warmth that he had felt only once before—sometime back—went through his body. It was at that exact moment that *Nick Stewart remembered everything!* He recognized Maureen and, he remembered where he had met Dr. Anthony Martin before. It all came flooding back to him!! His mind drifted back. How could he have forgotten?

Nicholas Stewart was in a hospital in England, after a car crash some months back. He was unconscious. That was the first time he saw Maureen—and Dr. Martin. He saw them in what he first believed was only a dream. They brought him back from a very dark place! He was badly hurt. It was the figures of Maureen and Anthony Martin that brought him out of a coma! Nick Stewart trembled as he remembered. This couldn't be.

There was another time, too—when he was praying for Alexandra—when he didn't know if she would live or die. He was praying that he wouldn't lose her, as he had his first wife. Dr. Martin was there—in the Chapel with him. He told Nick that Alex would live. Then, he said he was worried about Nick…He told him that he had to learn to forgive himself…that he had to find God again. It had changed his life!

Nicholas thought, at the time, they were figments of his imagination. Now, he knew they had been there…and they were *REAL!* At least, he thought they were. *Who,* or *What* were they? Were they *angels*? Nicholas knew the answer.

John was saying something to him that brought Nick back to the present.

"I told Maureen that you two are just alike. So, what do you think, Nick?"

"I told you, John. I think I'm probably in pretty good company."

Nick knew he was staring at Maureen. He tried to look away, but then he looked back at John's nurse. She smiled at him, and he knew he couldn't say anything to his friend about who he thought she might be. Everyone would think he was crazy, anyway.

Maureen turned John's sheets down and fixed his bed. She helped him back into bed, as she turned to Nick Stewart.

"I've been fortunate to be assigned to Mr. Cabe, as his 'Special Duty' nurse."

"Did you hear that, Nick? She's 'fortunate'. You don't know how much grief I've given this woman. She has to be a *Saint* to put up with me."

Both Maureen and Nick smiled. John didn't realize how close he was to the truth.

"I'm very glad to meet you, Maureen. I've heard good things about you—not only from John, but also from Matthew Clark, the little boy in the children's wing. He told me you bought him a model airplane. I just helped him assemble it."

"Matthew. He's a darlin'child."

Her Irish accent was unmistakable and her auburn hair glistened in the sunlight that was streaming in John's window. Nick couldn't take his eye off of her. Was he wrong? She looked real—he couldn't be wrong. There was a light around her—a warmth when she touched him—anyone could see that—anyone but John!

John interrupted.

"You're the one that bought him the model? He showed it to me. I promised him a ride on my plane, when I get out of this place."

"Oh, John, that's wonderful. You must have made his day. The child has been through so much—now, he has to be placed in a foster home when he's released. He doesn't know that yet."

"Doesn't he have any relatives at all?" asked Nick.

"We haven't been able to find anyone. His parent's relatives are either deceased or unable to be found. I'm glad you met him, John— and you too, Mr. Stewart."

If Nick was going to believe in angels, he knew somehow that this was all part of God's plan and somehow, Matthew Clark fit right into it!

Matthew and he were meant to meet. Matthew wanted to be a pilot—who else would he introduce the child to but—John? And, Kate Walcott? Was she a major player in this cast of characters, too?

Nick smiled a half-smile, half-grin. Only Alexandra, his wife, would believe him. Nick Stewart was determined to find Anthony Martin, M.D. He had to know and, he had to see the rest of this hospital. He had to find out for himself—was *Saints Hospital* just that?

Chapter Six

Kate Walcott was allowed to get up from her bed and sit in a wheelchair. It had been weeks—it felt like months. She had not looked in a mirror yet. She knew what she would see. Dr. Martin had, at her request, covered the mirrors in the bathroom. He told her there would be some scarring on the right side of her face. Still, he remained optimistic about more possible skin grafts.

Her face was still medicated with bandages. She reached up with her left hand and touched her forehead. The bandages covered most of the right side of her face. She wondered if she were going to be able to see out of her right eye. *It would serve me right, if I couldn't see. Mr. Cabe can't see...out of either eye.* Kate cried. He was blind and it was because of her.

She felt her mouth and her chin with her hand. They seemed to be intact, at least. She still couldn't move her right arm well, and the baths hurt so much. She was in pain most of the time, but the meds and drugs helped. She was able to move around a little now. She could push with her left arm and hand in the wheelchair, but it took so long—the blasted wheelchair wanted to go in circles.

Joseph had pushed her chair over by the window, but she didn't want to look at the outside scenery. It was too painful, remembering.

"Why didn't he just let me die?" she asked, knowing the answer.

John Cabe, according to Maureen, was not the kind of person to let another die—not without trying to rescue them.

She turned at the sound of footsteps entering her room. It was Dr. Martin. He had been kind to her but she didn't feel like talking right now. He walked toward her, her chart in his hand.

"Good afternoon, Kate. I thought you might want Nurse McConnell to come in and brush your hair for you. Today's going to be a better day for you, I promise."

"No baths? No physical therapy?" she replied bitterly. "That's the only thing that might make it better."

"I'm sorry. You have to have the baths and the therapy, Kate. You know that. I'm ready to take this bandage off the lower part of your arm. I want to see how the skin grafts are doing. Don't worry. I'll be gentle."

Kate flinched before Dr. Martin was even close to her. The thought of removing the bandages again—it had hurt so much!

Dr. Martin smiled at her. He touched her arm. His hand felt cool to the touch. He began to unwind the first bandage. Kate didn't look down. She just watched his face. The lower bandage came off and she didn't feel any pain. She looked down. Her arm looked bad, but it was smoother, not terrible. It was more red and bruised than anything. She looked back at Dr. Martin. He was nodding.

"It's okay. You don't have to look at it. It looks worse than it will, later. Kate, it's healing. I know it looks bad to you, but it's healing. You will probably have to have more surgery later, but I think you'll regain full use of this arm. I wasn't so sure a few days ago."

"What about my face?"

She faltered with the words when she asked him.

"I'm not ready to take off any bandages, yet. It has to heal a few more days. Don't worry, Kate. We'll take care of it, too. Would you like to look at yourself, now? The only thing you'll see right now is a pretty girl with a bandage on one side of her face."

Dr. Martin handed her a small mirror. She hesitated, and then held it up before her face. He was right. The left side of her face was untouched. Her mouth and chin were okay, too. It would be different, on the other side, without the bandages. She didn't want to see it without the bandage—not ever!

"Now, can I have Maureen come in and help you brush that beautiful hair? I believe that she even has a lipstick for you."

Kate smiled for the first time since she had been admitted to Saint's Hospital.

"I would like her to come in. I want to look better, this time. I want to go and see Mr. Cabe. I want her to take me there. I have to talk to him, just once more. Please, Dr. Martin—I have to see him."

Anthony Martin knew that John Cabe wasn't quite as ready for Katherine Walcott as she was for him. Still, the girl was so desperate. Perhaps, if Mr. Stewart stayed in the room with them—he had to pray about this.

"I'll let you know, Kate. I'll have Maureen come in to help you. I'll have to talk to Mr. Cabe first."

"Please, see if he will talk to me today."

Kate's hopes were draining.

"I'll see. I'll let you know, one way or the other. Try not to worry."

It was no surprise to Dr. Martin when he found Nicholas Stewart waiting in his office. He expected him. He was ready for him.

"Mr. Stewart," he said, "I think we have quite a lot to talk about, don't we?"

"Dr. Martin? Or, should I even call you by that name? I just remembered where I met you—and your 'nurse'. Maybe we should begin with that?"

"Of course."

Anthony Martin sat down behind his desk, motioning Nick to one of the chairs on the other side. Nicholas Stewart needed answers. Now, it was time for Dr. Anthony Martin to place his trust in a human being.

"I wasn't certain you existed, until today," Nick continued. "I do know you changed my life that last time that we spoke. How is this possible? Or, am I dreaming right now?"

Dr. Martin smiled.

"I think you already know, Nicholas. Your physical being just doesn't want to accept it yet. It is true. We do exist. Only a few are able to actually see or recognize us—later. You're one of those He has chosen."

Nick swallowed hard. Suddenly, he had nothing to say.

"You've always wondered, in the back of your mind, if we were real, ever since your *own* accident. We were there, with you—through that trauma and then again, when Alexandra was hurt.

"That's what we do, you see—our unit here. *We search for those souls who are suffering the most traumas—the ones who are struggling with life-changing events—emotional, as well as physical ones.*

"All the people in this hospital are at that stage of their life, Nicholas. They are either going to accept God and His mercies, or not—it's their choice. We are simply putting the right people into their lives—at the right time. Some of them won't get another chance. Some are dying. Some will refuse to take the risk—and for some, it will *change their lives forever!*

"With you, Nicholas, the right person was Alexandra—and with her, it was you. You chose life—to come back and live, really live. But, do you remember your friends at that time? John and Mac played a really important part at that stage of your life.

"Now it's John's turn. He's ready. He needs a change in his life. He needs to find God in order to *forgive*—in order to truly love."

Nick was quiet. He remembered what had happened in his past. He was struggling with forgiving himself back then. He could never have given Alexandra his entire being, if he hadn't done that first. Dr. Martin had been there to remind him—so had Maureen. It was then that he re-dedicated himself to God and his life changed forever...

"What can I do to help him?" he asked.

"Believe me Nicholas. You're doing it. You've already asked God to guide you. He will."

"And Kate Walcott? Is she a part of this?"

"You know that already. Yes, Kate has a great need too. She's at a crossroads herself. Mr. Cabe found her at just the right time. She tried to kill herself, you know."

"I heard."

"There's a reason for that, Nicholas. Mr. Cabe has to find out that reason. He may be the only one left that Kate will tell. That's what we have to encourage. They need to communicate. I think your Alexandra may be able to help Mr. Cabe. She has a great influence on him. But, you already know that, too."

"Alex should be here day after tomorrow, Dr. Martin. However, this is an awful lot to take in."

"Alexandra will understand. She'll believe you, Nicholas, because she believes in you. You need to talk to her before she sees Mr. Cabe."

Nick Stewart found himself mesmerized by Anthony Martin. He couldn't say no. He had to help John and Kate—and Matthew, where did Matthew fit in this unequal equation?

"I'll speak to Alex. I'd like to see the rest of your hospital, if I may?"

"Of course. Let's go. Prepare yourself, Nicholas. Some of the things you see may be difficult to understand."

Alexandra Stewart got off the small aircraft that landed in Clarksville. Her blonde hair blew across her face as she walked from the plane to the small terminal building. She was excited and happy. Nick would be inside, waiting for her.

She had missed him, even though it had been only a few days. She went to the baggage claim, and looked around for her husband. Then, she saw him, walking toward her. His face lit up when he found her in the small crowd. He rushed over and picked her up off the floor, giving her a kiss that made the other passengers turn and stare at them.

"I've missed you so much," he said, as he returned her to the floor.

"Wow! If I knew that I'd get that kind of reception, I would have stayed away a few more days!"

She felt a little dizzy and lightheaded.

It must be from the flight.

Alexandra held onto Nick, feeling safe just being near him.

"I love you, Alexandra," he said.

The tone of his voice was sobering. Something was wrong—she heard it.

"I love you too, darling. What's going on?"

"You know me too well."

Just as Nick couldn't explain the angels, he could never explain the connection that he and his wife had. It was as if they knew what the other would say before it happened, and almost as if she could read his mind.

"Is it John?"

"I think we better head for the Coffee Shoppe. This is one story that may take awhile. Here, let me get your luggage."

Nick got her suitcases, as Alexandra watched him. Then, he put his other arm around her waist and led her to the Airport Coffee Shoppe.

Nick Stewart watched his wife's face change from one of skepticism to awe and wonder, as he told her about Dr. Anthony Martin and Maureen McConnell.

"The hospital—it's amazing, Alex," he continued.

"They have machines and technology that haven't been invented by man yet, Alexandra."

"How can it be possible, Nick?"

"You have to believe me. Do you remember anything about when you were in the hospital in California? Did you—did you see anyone—?"

"I don't remember. I remember seeing people in white, telling me it was time to return—and it was so fuzzy when I came out from under the anesthesia. I remember seeing you—and John—and knowing everything was going to be all right."

Nick was slightly disappointed. He thought Alex would remember something more.

"I was hoping your memory was as clear as mine," he said.

"I believe you, Nicholas," she whispered.

"What? What did you say?"

"I said I believe you. I know you darling. I know *you*. I believe you and I believe we have to do what Dr. Martin says to help John."

"Oh, Alex, you're—I love you. Thank you for believing me and not thinking I'm crazy."

"We both know God works in ways that man may not always understand, Nick. Look at us—who would ever believe how we got together?"

As always, she put his mind at ease. Alexandra was always there for him—his partner, his love—his soul mate.

"Now, I think I've had enough coffee for three people. Can we go see John?"

"Of course."

He pulled her to him as they got up, and he kissed her again. He didn't care who was watching them. He loved her. The world could know it!

Kate Walcott was disappointed when Dr. Martin didn't return. She wanted to talk to John Cabe. She wanted to tell him what had happened to her—before the accident. She wasn't sure if she could ever tell another soul, but *he had to know.* If Dr. Martin didn't return by this evening, she would take matters into her own hands.

When Alexandra and Nick walked into Saints Hospital, Nick took her first to see the painting. Alex stood in front of the picture, gazing at the face of the angel that the artist had pictured.

"It's beautiful," she said. "Look at her face. She looks like a Saint."

"It's like the person John described to me. He thinks his nurse looks like this, Alex. She hasn't told him any different. But, wait until you see the real thing. You may remember her, Alexandra. I'm sure you will. I just know both she and Dr. Martin were there with you when you almost died."

"I'm ready—let's go see John."

They walked together to John Cabe's room.

"John? Hey Bud, I've brought a surprise for you."

Nick went into the room, holding his wife's hand and pulling her close behind him.

"Hi, Nick, what's the surprise?"

John was sitting up in his chair. He looked as charming as ever to Alexandra Stewart. She walked over to him and kissed his cheek.

"Hi, John. What's this I hear about you having another woman looking out for you?"

"Alexandra! Oh, Alex…I'm so glad you're here."

John hugged his friend.

"Did you bring Sabrina?"

"No, I'm sorry. We may fly her down for the weekend, but she's in school. I had her friend, Marguerite, keep her for a few days."

"Still—you're here. You and Nick and Mac are here. It's so good."

John was overwhelmed as Alexandra put her arms around him.

"It's going to be okay, John. Please believe that—believe *me.*"

Maureen had told him the same thing and he had believed her. He certainly believed Alexandra. She would *never* lie to him.

"Hey, beautiful, you know I'd believe anything you tell me," he said to her.

Alex smiled when he called her "beautiful." It had always been his nickname for her. She looked up at Nick, who was smiling down at both of them.

He nodded to her. She was what John needed most right now. She was the one he would talk to.

"Well, John," Alex continued, "tell me about that cat. I have to see him. I think Nick and I are going to stay at your ranch tonight, if you don't mind."

"Mind? You know you're welcome. Just be prepared for a man's housekeeping, Alex. Maybe you can give it a woman's touch."

"I'll try. Now, tell me how you're feeling. Nick's going to get us all some soft drinks while you and I talk, but I want to hear everything."

Alex glanced at Nicholas and motioned for him to leave them alone, just as he had asked her to do. He told John that he would be back in a few minutes.

John was silent for awhile. He had always been able to talk to Alexandra. He didn't know why it was so difficult now. He knew he had to talk to someone or he'd explode.

He finally opened up to Alex, just as Nick and Dr. Martin had hoped.

"I'm scared, Alex," he began. "I'm so afraid!"

"I would be frightened too, John. Of course you're scared."

"I don't want to be blind. I want to see. Why did God do this to me, Alexandra? Why?"

"I asked myself that question, John. I don't have an answer. I do know He'll see you through this, if you let Him. It's going to be easy to blame Him, John, but He didn't do this to you, my dear, dear friend. No matter what you believe right now, believe what I'm going to tell you.

"He's the One who will save you. He loves you so much, John. He loves you more than Nick and I love you. He will bring you through this, John."

John Cabe listened. He didn't quite expect what Alex said to him, but he listened to her. She was so adamant about God's love for him.

"John?" she asked, "Have you seen Kate Walcott?"

"Yes, I spoke to her. Why does everyone ask me that? It hasn't helped, Alex."

"Perhaps if you let *her* talk—and tell you what made her want to take that terrible way out. I know it's difficult for you, John. I would stay in the room with you if I could, when you talk to her, but I don't think she would open up with anyone else there."

"You think she'll open up—to me?"

"I do. You're such a good man, John Cabe. We love you so much. If I didn't think that it was good for you, not Kate—*you*—I would never suggest it."

"But, why, Alex—why?"

"Because you *hate* her, John. You hate her and you even hate yourself. You have to face that—face her. In doing that, perhaps you'll find you might be able to forgive her—and that's what will help you."

Alexandra was holding his hand. He was clinging to hers as if his very life depended on it.

Alex prayed. *Please help him Lord, he's so afraid.*

Alexandra found she wasn't certain that this would help him if he didn't want to do this on his own, but it was what both Nick and Dr. Martin had asked of her. She knew it had to work. She had learned to trust in Nick and Nick trusted God, as she did. Now, she had to pass that trust along to John Cabe.

"You saved my life once, John," she continued, "Let me save yours, now."

Tears were rolling down both their cheeks. Alex put her face close to his and he could feel her tears mingle with his own. He knew how much she cared—and he trusted her.

"I'll do it, Alex. I'll try to listen and hear what she says this time."

Nick Stewart stood just outside John's door for the last few minutes. He listened to them and prayed. His own eyes were moist. When he walked back in, he went over to his best friend and his wife.

"John? I'd like to pray for you, if you'll let me."

He took his friend's hand, and kneeled in front of him, holding Alexandra's hand in his other one. In this small circle, they lifted a prayer to the God of healing and love.

Dr. Anthony Martin stopped in the corridor of the hospital. He was uncertain what to tell Katherine Walcott. She had seemed so desperate when he saw her before. She had already attempted suicide once and she was still so vulnerable.

He hoped that Alexandra Stewart was able to speak to John Cabe.

Neither she nor Nick had sought him out yet to tell him what was happening. He had to trust his instincts about them. They would do the right thing for their friend. Dr. Martin knocked on Kate Walcott's door.

"Dr. Martin," the girl exclaimed, "what did he say?"

"Katherine, you have to be patient. Mr. Cabe will let us know when he's ready to see you. You need to think about him—what he's feeling. Can you do that?"

Kate Walcott was not a patient woman. Dr. Martin did have a point, though. John Cabe was certainly worse off than she was. She was being selfish to ask him to speak with her—on demand.

Why did she think that it would matter to him, anyway? She took a deep breath and tried to relax and then she told Dr. Martin that she would wait.

As Anthony Martin opened her door to leave, he almost ran over John Cabe's wheelchair. Behind him, pushing his chair, was Alexandra Stewart.

Dr. Martin smiled, and held out his hand to her. As Alex extended hers, and as their hands touched, Alex Stewart was certain that she had made the right decision.

"Katherine, this is Mr. Nick Stewart's wife, Alexandra. I think you already know Mr. Cabe."

Katherine Walcott turned to meet Alexandra Stewart, and Alex gasped when she saw her. The right side of Kate's face was covered, but the side that Alex saw was beautiful and almost an exact twin to the Saint in the picture she had seen downstairs!

"I'm happy to meet you, Mrs. Stewart. Mr. Cabe, I'm so glad you came back."

Alex was too stunned to say much. She nodded to the young woman, and then told Dr. Martin that she needed to return to her husband, but that John wanted to visit for awhile with Kate Walcott.

"Of course, I'll walk you down the hall, Alex."

Dr. Martin seemed to sense her confusion.

"Will you be all right, John?" Alex asked.

"Yes, Alex. I'd like to spend some time with Miss Walcott alone, if that's all right?"

Katherine Walcott was grateful to him and she knew it was time to speak the truth.

"I'd like that very much, Mr. Cabe. Thank you."

"I'm confused, Dr. Martin," said Alex.

"I can imagine, Alexandra. You're taking a lot on faith, aren't you?"

"Faith? Yes, and trust—trust in my husband, and my God."

"Do you remember when that was the biggest issue in your life—trusting again?"

Alexandra heard Anthony Martin remind her of her own life—back to when she felt she could never trust any man, ever again. Then, along came Nicholas—Nicholas, who waited and waited—just for her. Nicholas—who earned her trust again. How did Dr. Martin know about that?

She looked directly into the physician's eyes. She was always able to "read" people through their eyes. When she did this, she saw the truest compassion she had ever seen.

"Alexandra, because you trust—you're about to be entrusted with something so precious that you won't believe it. Don't ever doubt. Miracles do happen."

He held out his hand to her, and Alex touched her fingers to his. In that moment, she knew why Nicholas Stewart trusted him. He walked her back to John Cabe's room, where her own true love waited for her.

"Alex? Are you all right?" Nick asked her.

Nick Stewart hadn't seen that look on his wife's face in some time. He wasn't sure if she was afraid—or just in awe. He chose the latter, when he saw her glance back at Dr. Martin.

"I'm fine, darling," she answered.

Alex felt a little queasy and she was slightly dizzy again. She didn't know whether to laugh or cry. Instead, she changed the subject. She realized that she did a lot of that recently.

"Nick, I thought you said John described his nurse, Maureen, as the one who looks like the angel in the picture downstairs."

"I did. But, she doesn't. Why? Did you meet her?"

"No, Nicholas. I met Kate Walcott, and she's a *dead ringer* for the angel in that picture! So, how many are there, Dr. Martin?"

Anthony Martin laughed, a laugh that came from deep inside and rose to caress them.

"I'll try and explain. You see, John asked Maureen what she looked like. Then, Maureen asked for John to *describe* her. He did. John described a woman that he wished she would look like—a woman that he could fall in love with!

"But, I saw Maureen. She doesn't look much like..."

"She's not the woman your friend described to you, Mr. Stewart. She's what he wants her to look like. Maureen is a kind and gentle soul, but the woman John Cabe described—the woman he has in mind—that woman is Kate Walcott!

"Maureen—well, you both have an idea of who she is—of who I am. Is it so hard to believe we can take a human form?"

"It's mind boggling—too much for us 'humans'," replied Nick.

"Way too much," agreed Alexandra.

"I know. The two of you would never have been trusted with this information, if we didn't know where your spirit, soul and hearts are."

"And John? Is he going to be all right?" asked Alex.

"It's up to him now. We can't impose. We just place the people together."

Nick found he was holding on tightly to his wife, drawing her closer to him. He felt as he had when he first met her. He wanted to protect her. He wasn't sure from what. What if he had chosen the wrong way, when Dr. Martin visited him? But, he hadn't. He had chosen *LIFE—and Alexandra!*

Chapter Seven

It was so quiet after Alexandra and Dr. Martin closed the door, that John Cabe wasn't certain where Kate Walcott was sitting in the room. He stopped and listened for her breathing.

"Miss Walcott?" he asked

"I'm sorry, Mr. Cabe. I'm over here."

Kate moved her wheelchair next to him and took his hand. He could feel her tremble.

"I was just so surprised that you agreed to see me. I'm very grateful, Mr. Cabe."

"My name's John. You can call me that. It's okay."

He wasn't comfortable, but he sensed the young woman was a lot more uncomfortable than he was. He tried to remember what Alexandra had asked him to do. He needed to listen.

"I go by Kate. My mother named me Katherine—Katherine B. Walcott. It's her name too. I'm from Massachusetts originally."

"Oh, so what were you doing in Arizona—a vacation?"

"No, nothing like that."

Kate became still.

John didn't know what to say to her, so he sat quietly until she continued. He heard her take in a deep breath.

"I followed a man here, Mr. Cabe—John. It turned out to be the biggest mistake of my life."

John swallowed hard. This was the big secret? A boyfriend turned her down? John squirmed in his seat. He was more uncomfortable than before! That's the big reason she tried to kill herself—that's why I'm sitting here, unable to see?

He was disgusted but he thought of what Alex said to him and he kept his mouth shut as Kate Walcott continued.

"You see, I trusted him. He was my stepfather, and he left my mother about a month ago. I followed him to see if he'd come back. I was going to talk him into it."

Kate Walcott's voice was quivering. John suspected she was crying. This was not what he expected to hear. He leaned forward—toward her voice.

"Go on, Kate."

"When I found him, he was nice enough. He sounded like he was considering returning to my mother. We had dinner and I asked to talk with him some more. He suggested that we needed to go someplace quieter—so when he asked me back to his hotel room, I never stopped to think—I—I, oh, it's so hard."

Her voice broke. It was becoming more and more difficult for her to speak. John instinctively reached for her hand again.

She has such small hands.

"It's okay. Take your time. Kate. Take all the time that you need."

John had not planned comforting her. He was angry with her. Why did she make it so difficult for him to stay that way?

Then, she said what he dreaded hearing, but suspected when the tone of her voice changed before.

"He raped me, John."

"What?"

"He raped me."

John tensed. *What had she been through? Her own stepfather? What hell she must have been going through—now the crash, and her burns.* His mind was whirling and all of a sudden, John Cabe felt an anger he had never felt before. It was directed toward this unknown monster who had done this to her!

It was no wonder she attempted to kill herself. He didn't know what to say to her. He clutched her hand and held it tightly against his chest, as Kate's tears dropped on both of them.

"It will be all right, Kate. Somehow, it will be all right again."

"I don't understand how God could let it happen," she cried.

John understood that pain. He was asking the same question. He had no answer for her. He just put his arms around her, and he let her cry.

Alex and Nick walked down to the hospital Cafeteria, where they found Mac waiting for them.

"Alexandra! How are you, darling girl?"

"Hi, Mac. I'm pretty well. Sabrina sends you a kiss."

"Have you seen our John yet?"

"We just came from there," answered Nick.

He pulled out a chair for Alex and they both sat down with Mac.

"We were wondering. Do you want to ride with us to his ranch? We're going to spend the night out there. He has three bedrooms and that cottage that's behind the main house, so there's plenty of room."

"Sure. I'll take the cottage and you folks take the house. Maybe I can find that old cat of his. He can keep me company."

Nick had to laugh. Alex squeezed his hand and looked over at her husband. She loved his laugh. She had always loved it. Both of them were in a more optimistic mood about John than they had been an hour ago.

There was nothing more that they could do tonight. John had not come back from Kate's room, so they left a message with Joseph, telling him that they'd be back in the morning and to let Mr. Cabe know.

Alex found she was tired from the flight. She had a slight upset stomach and she wanted to unpack. She was also anxious to be alone with Nicholas. These strange mood swings weren't like her. They had just developed recently—she was either on top of the world, or crying at the drop of a hat. She missed her husband—that was probably all it was.

Soon, Mac and Nick found the car, picked up Alexandra, and the three headed toward John Cabe's ranch.

John Cabe was still holding Kate. He tried to comfort her, but she cried until he believed there could be no more tears. He tried to find some tissues for her, but had no idea where they were kept. She tried to speak, as if reading his thoughts.

"I'm so sorry. I have to get some tissues."

She moved away from him and he listened to her wheelchair move to the other side of the room. He heard her pull the tissues out of the box, and then she came back, sitting even closer to him.

"I can't imagine what you think of me now, John," she whispered.

Her voice was softer than before, and John could barely hear her.

"I don't think anything, Kate, except that you've been through hell. If I could change things—for both of us—I would. Now, we have to decide what we can do from here on out."

"I have to do something to help you, Mr. Cabe—John. I'll do anything. When you get out of here, I could come and cook, or clean for you. I could help you. I know I could."

"Whoa there—not so fast, *Beautiful*..."

He couldn't believe he said that! He had called her by Alexandra's nickname. He vaguely remembered the woman he had dragged from the crash. She looked about twenty-three or four years old. He remembered that she had auburn hair—and that she was extremely pretty.

He didn't know how the burns had affected her. She had been burned on her arm and shoulder. Her face had been burned too. He wondered what she looked like now.

"I'm sorry," she said, "I didn't mean to push like that. I'm not a very patient woman, I guess."

Kate knew it was one of her major flaws.

"It's Okay," he replied. "I just meant we're both going to be here for awhile. I want you to get well, Kate. You may have a long road ahead. How are the burns? Are you having therapy? What about this 'secret' you've had to keep? Have you told anyone else what that monster did to you? Did you tell the police?"

He realized he had just *bombarded* her with questions. John couldn't help feeling protective. He had lived around Nick Stewart too long. They were both men who took care of their women. It was old-fashioned, he knew. That's just the way they had been raised.

"You're the only one I've told, except for Maureen, my nurse," she replied.

"You didn't report it? Were you checked out at all?"

"The wreck—it happened before I could do anything—now, I just can't. Maureen told Dr. Martin and he took some medical tests, but I can't give the police a report, John. I just can't!"

He knew what the girl would have to go through. He could understand her reluctance to give police a report of what had happened to her. At least, she was given medical care. He wondered if Dr. Martin reported it. It was a law, so police might already know. If they did, they would be contacting Kate when she was better.

Maureen and Alexandra were right—he couldn't hate her now. He hated the man who did this to her—to them. He was the real perpetrator. He had caused her crash—and in a way, he had caused John's blindness, too.

He knew that Kate had to identify him and give a report to the Sheriff, even if she couldn't do it now. She had to—for both of their sakes.

"Kate, I know you can't face this yet, but you have to report what happened. If you meant what you said—that you'd do anything for me, that's the one thing I want you to do. Talk to the Sheriff, as soon as you're up to it. Promise me."

Kate Walcott never thought he would ask this much from her. She had told him the truth—something she couldn't easily do. But, he had risked so much for her—look at him. *He's blind and he's still thinking of me.* Kate kept repeating that. She took a deep breath and squeezed his hand.

"If that's what I must do, I promise. I promise I'll talk to the Sheriff, John."

John squeezed her hand. He was suddenly very tired. He had to rest.

"Kate, I'm sorry. I have to lie down. I'll come back later, if you want. Or, you come visit me. Say, what about dinner? You come on down to my room. We'll ask Maureen to bring your tray down there. We can visit more then, Okay?"

"All right, John. Are you sure?"

"I'm sure. You go rest. You've had so much stress, Kate. Maybe you can sleep a little better now—this afternoon."

"Thank you, John."

He didn't know why, but when she said his name, it gave him chills—and not the cold chills that he had felt before!

"Rest, Kate. I hope you can nap."

"I will. You do the same."

John Cabe forgot that he had not called for assistance. He wasn't certain he could make it back to his room, after he left Kate's room. Then, he felt a hand on his shoulder.

"Need a ride back?"

Maureen McConnell was right behind him. John smiled. She was right on time.

Nick, Alex and Mac pulled up at John's ranch and, as Nick went to check the mail, Alex and Mac walked up on the front porch of the main house.

"It's pretty out here," Alex said to Mac.

"It is peaceful. Did you see a yellow cat anywhere?"

"No. John's cat?"

"Old Yeller," laughed Mac. "He'll be around here at suppertime, I imagine. He's usually in that chair, waiting for us."

"Old Yeller?" laughed Alex. "I can't imagine John Cabe having a cat."

"When you see this one, you'll understand."

Nick climbed the porch steps and sat down on the top one.

"The neighbors must have picked up the mail. Where's the cat?"

Alex looked at Mac and smiled. She had to see this animal of John's. Not only had Mac talked about him, but now, Nick? He must be some cat...

"Well, are we ready to go inside? I need a shower, guys."

"Sure, Babe—Mac, you have the key to the cottage?"

"Yeah, right here. By the way, I picked up some groceries and put them in the frig. Thought we might need something to eat later. I picked up some things for breakfast too."

"Thanks, Mac. I'll give you a call later. If you got eggs and milk, I may whip up one of my famous omelets—the 'Nick Stewart Special'."

"That's a deal. I'll put Alexandra's luggage inside, then go on to the cottage."

Nick and Alexandra walked inside the ranch house.

"It's not bad," said Nick. "John's fixed the place up a lot. The cottage where Mac's going to stay used to be the main house."

"It's so peaceful. No wonder he loves it here."

Alex walked from the large living room into the kitchen. Then, she went to the hallway, just past the large stone fireplace. She checked out the bedrooms and the baths.

"You know Nick, it's similar to our home in Colorado. It's really roomier than it looks. The bedrooms are nice too. I think I'll take that shower, now. Do you mind putting on a pot of coffee for us?"

"You've got it, Babe."

Alex unpacked some of her suitcase, grabbed a clean set of jeans, a shirt and headed for the shower. When she stepped out of the bath, she could smell the aroma of the coffee. She put on a robe instead of her clothes, and walked into the living room, where Nick was reading the local paper.

"Finally," she whispered, 'alone'."

She walked over to her husband and sat down across from him, then grabbed the paper from him, and tossed it on the floor. Nick just smiled at her, got up, and walked over to her. He picked her up, and carried her into the bedroom.

"I love you, Mrs. Stewart," he said.

"Same here, Mr. Stewart."

She looked down at him, and kissed her husband's face, as he closed the door.

It was nearly dinnertime. John Cabe had slept almost an hour, after returning to his room. When he awoke, he remembered that he had promised to check on Matthew Clark. He hadn't done that yet. He buzzed for Maureen or Joseph. He needed to get to the Children's Wing.

"Yes, Mr. Cabe?"

It was Joseph who answered. John asked him to take him to check on Matthew. Joseph pushed John's wheelchair down the hall to where the children were.

"They're all in a group play session right now, Mr. Cabe. We can go in and listen. I think they have a leader. They're probably singing, or having a story time. I'll find Matthew and bring him over next to you, so you can sit with him."

"Thank you, Joseph."

John could hear the voices of the children. It was a pleasant sound, and he liked what he heard. When Joseph wheeled him through the doors, into some kind of large auditorium, the voices grew even louder. Someone was playing a piano, and he heard a woman's voice leading the songs.

"Now everyone, we're going to learn a new song. I'm going to have Paul play it first on the piano, and then I'll give you the words. Then, we'll all try it together, okay?"

John was sure it was Maureen. He listened as the melody was played on the piano. Maureen then sang the first lyric. Her voice was beautiful, as he was certain it would be. Then, all the kids joined in. It sounded like a choir of angels to John Cabe. He felt a small chubby hand slip into his large one at that moment.

"Hi, John."

It was Matthew. John Cabe shook the child's hand and smiled.

"Hi, Matthew. How are you doing today?"

"Fine. How are you, John?"

"I'm okay. Hey, the song's really nice. Are you singing?"

"Yeah. I do pretty well. I get a little off-key once in awhile, but nobody seems to mind. They just want you to try. Can you sing?"

John Cabe laughed. It was the first time he felt like laughing in a long time.

"That's not one of my strong suites, Matthew. I like to listen to music, but I'm afraid singing isn't one of my gifts."

"Well, you can sing with me, John. I don't care what you sound like."

Matthew squeezed John's hand and went on to sing at the top of his lungs. John smiled, as the boy tried to hit a high note and his voice didn't quite make it. John started humming along and kept time with his foot. At the end of the song, everyone was clapping as if it were the best music in the world. John found he was clapping, too. He had actually enjoyed it!

After the music ended, John asked Matthew if he would like to come back and visit in his room—maybe have a bite of supper with him and—"a new friend." John didn't know how Kate might feel, but he believed that Matthew would be able to cheer up anyone. Matthew jumped at the chance. He said he was tired of "just being with the kids," and he told John he was older than a lot of them. John laughed again.

Maureen McConnell saw John enter the room with Joseph, and she smiled when she saw Matthew and John leave together.

"Things couldn't be going better," she whispered.

Kate was glad to get the truth out, and she was glad that John Cabe had asked her to see him again. She was determined to help him in some way. She couldn't go back home—not now, maybe not ever. She would never be able to face her mother. Her mother would never believe what had happened to her.

Kate felt the tears coming again. She had to stop this! She put on some lipstick and buzzed for an aide to transport her to John's room.

John ordered three dinner trays and asked Matthew if he would move the small table near them, so they could all eat together.

"Who else is coming?" asked Matthew.

"A nice lady," replied John.

"She's had a rough time, Matthew, so we may need to cheer her up a little, okay?"

"Okay, I'll try."

The child was used to some of the patients in this hospital. He had been here for quite awhile, and knew that most of the people here had been badly hurt in some way or another.

He thought about his own Mom and Dad. Matthew didn't cry much anymore. He knew they were never coming back. Still, he thought he saw them every now and then. It was almost like they were still worrying about him—like they were still watching over him—and it made him feel better, especially at night.

"Okay, John, the table's moved. It's right in front of you, and to the right."

The child knew to tell me just where the furniture was placed. The boy's smart. I wonder if he thinks a lot about his parents.

At that moment, Joseph brought in the dinner trays.

"Just put them on our table, here. Thanks a lot, Joseph."

"Miss Walcott is just outside the door, Mr. Cabe. Shall I tell her to come on in?"

"She's the person we're waiting for," said John.

Joseph wheeled Kate into the room. She saw John first, then

Matthew.

"Hello, John. It's Kate. Hi, young man."

"Kate, this is Matthew Clark. I asked him to eat with us. I hope you don't mind. He's my newest friend. Matthew, this is Kate, the lady I told you about."

Kate and Matthew looked each other over.

"I'm glad you're here, Matthew. You're looking good. How are you feeling?"

Kate was uncertain what to say to the child. She wasn't sure what was wrong with him.

"I'm fine. I've been here quite a while, so I'm really tired of the hospital."

"I hope you're able to go home soon, Matthew."

John could have kicked himself. He should have told her about Matthew's parents before he got them together.

"Hey guys—dinner's getting cold. I told Matthew that you and I would take him back to the Children's Wing after supper, Kate. Is that Okay?"

"Sure, John. Mmmm, the food smells good. Let's see what we have?"

Matthew looked with surprise at the food.

"These are hamburgers! Hey, that's great. We *never* have hamburgers. John, do you need some help?"

The child had thought to ask John if he needed help, and Kate Walcott felt as if she should have thought of it too. She went over next to John, and handed him a fork.

"John, most of this is finger food but, they haven't put anything on the burgers. I'd be glad to add what you want. There's mustard and mayonnaise—which do you like?"

"Just show me where it is on the plate, Kate. I have to learn. Matthew, why don't you go down to that soft drink machine and get us all some sodas. Here—-I've got some change. Take this and come right back. I think I'll take a Root Beer. How about you, Kate?"

"That sounds good to me. Get whatever you want, Matthew. Can you carry three cans? I'd be glad to help."

"I can get it. I'll be right back."

The child left the room, and John turned toward Kate's chair

"I'm sorry. I had to tell you—his parents died in a car wreck. I

74

should have told you before I introduced him. I didn't even think about it until you asked him about going home. He'll never go home, Kate."

"Oh, John—oh, that poor child. He's so darling, John. If you could see him…"

She fumbled with the words, and could have hit herself for saying that!

"It's okay, Kate. I'm getting used to hearing the word *see*. What does he look like?"

He had made it easy for her, again. John Cabe was a kind person. She tried once more.

"He's got reddish-brown hair. He has freckles and a chubby little face. His eyes are brown, like yours. He's not real thin, but he's going to be tall. You can tell. He looks a lot like—like…"

"Yes?"

"He looks a lot like you, John. He has your coloring. He's a fine looking boy."

John didn't know what to say. Matthew looked like him? Poor kid—but he was pleased when he heard Kate say it.

"Kate? What do you look like? I mean, what color are your eyes? I need to know who I'm speaking to. I don't have any other way to tell."

She went closer to him—and picked up his hand.

"My eyes are green, John."

She took his hand, and with her hand covering his, moved it down the side of her face that had not been burned. He was amazed as he tried to visualize this woman—long lashes, small nose, and the smoothest skin—and then, his fingers traced the outline of her mouth. It was so soft. He had never been this close to a woman, unless he had been serious about her. He let his fingers linger a moment on her lips. It was strange. It was as if Kate had the same features that he thought Maureen had, only without the Irish accent. He knew he was too close to her to think straight, and he drew his hand away.

He moved back, but Kate had already heard his breath catch, as he touched her face. Matthew came back with the soft drinks just at that time. He gave Kate her soda, and popped the top of the can for John.

"Root beers for all!"

"Thank you, Matthew."

Kate Walcott was glad, in one way, that the child had come back at that moment, but another part of her wished she could be alone longer with John Cabe.

"Let's eat," said John. "If I manage to make a mess, nobody say anything!"

He had made them laugh. They both accepted his blindness, and so had he.

Kate and Matthew talked almost nonstop at dinner. They both liked hamburgers with mustard, pickles and onions. Kate liked baseball, and so did Matthew. They loved planes and model aircraft. It seemed they had a lot more in common than they would have thought at first. Kate asked Matthew if he liked animals, and he said he did. He used to have a dog, but he didn't have a pet anymore. He also liked horses, and he thought he would like to have a cat someday.

Then, John told both of them about "Old Yeller," and they laughed at his stories. John asked both of them to come and visit his ranch when they got out of the hospital. He said that he knew Matthew would like the horses, and he had already promised him a plane ride. John was pleased when Kate told him that she rode too, and that she would like to ride the horses with Matthew, *if* that was okay with them.

It had been a nice evening for the three of them. John Cabe hadn't expected it to go that well, and gave most of the credit to Matthew. It was easy to talk to Kate Walcott with Matthew there. When it was time to take him back to the children's wing, Matthew pushed Kate's wheelchair while Joseph pushed John's. When they got to the Unit, Kate insisted tucking in Matthew. John went with her, to the child's bed.

"Goodnight, Matthew," she said. "I hope I can see more of you."

She tucked him in, and kissed the child's forehead.

"Goodnight, Kate. Thanks for everything," the child whispered.

"Matthew, I'll see you again, tomorrow."

"Okay John. Thanks for the dinner. You were right. She is a nice lady."

John grinned, and asked Joseph if he could walk behind Kate's chair and push her home.

"You'll have to give me directions, Kate—and you too, Joseph. I'll *walk you home, Kate,*" John smiled.

"I wish I could manage this thing by myself," Kate replied. "My one arm's not strong enough yet, so I just go in circles."

"We make quite a pair, don't we? I can't see where I'm going, and you go in circles."

Kate had to smile. She found John Cabe to be a delightful man, with a good sense of humor, in spite of the circumstances.

Joseph waited for John outside Kate's door. He told John and Kate that he would leave them alone for a moment, to say goodnight—just to call him when they needed him.

"That's awkward," Kate said, as Joseph stepped out of sight.

"Our chaperon," chuckled John.

"John, thank you for tonight. It was nice. The child—he's wonderful. I hope you don't mind if I see him again."

"Of course not! He needs all the friends he can get. He is a good kid, isn't he?"

"He is. Well, I better get ready for the night."

"Yes, and I better get back to my room, too. Are you going to be all right, Kate?"

She looked at John Cabe. She wished that he could *see* her—*but then, he'd see the bandages and the scars—still, she wished he could see—for HIS sake. Oh, God, what had she done to him?*

"I'll be fine, John. Maybe I'll see you tomorrow?"

She wanted to be with him again. She owed him her life, regardless what had happened, and it had cost him so much.

"Sure. Until tomorrow, then. Good night, Kate."

John called for Joseph, who was waiting just around the corner. He grinned at Kate, and led John back to his room.

As a nurse helped Kate into bed, she couldn't help but think of the man who had saved her life. She had told him everything she could never tell another soul. It *seemed to her* that he didn't *hate* her anymore—at least, he didn't show it. She wondered if it could be pity that he was feeling toward her. She hoped not. Kate closed her eyes and fell asleep, dreaming about John Cabe.

Chapter Eight

The weekend finally arrived for Nick and Alexandra, and they went to the airport to pick up their daughter, six-year-old Sabrina Stewart. Nick had the child flown into Clarksville on his private jet. He wanted her to be able to visit her "Uncle John" in the hospital, thinking that Sabrina could cheer up anyone!

Nick saw Sabrina's dark curls bouncing toward him. She skipped down the plane's corridor and into the reception area, where he and Alex were waiting for her. She spied her parents, and ran to them, jumping into Nick Stewart's waiting arms!

"Daddy! I missed you. Where's Uncle John?"

The child kissed her father on his cheek, and then wiggled out of his arms, getting down to go throw her arms around her mother's legs. Alexandra bent down and kissed her stepdaughter.

"Sabrina, I'm so glad you're here. I missed you so much."

Alexandra grabbed the child's hand, and Nick put his arm around his wife's waist, as they walked out of the airport, to a waiting car.

"Uncle Mac!"

Mac Timmons got out of the back seat of the car and swung the child into the waiting sedan with him.

"Hey there, sport! How's my favorite niece?"

"I'm fine. I got an "A" on my printing, Mom. Daddy, did you hear? I got an 'A'!"

Nick climbed into the driver's seat and turned back to look at his daughter. She had his hair and his blue eyes. She not only looked like him, she had some of his same idiosyncrasies. He grinned back at her.

"An 'A', huh? I guess that's pretty good. How about that, Alex?"

He winked at his wife.

"I'd say an 'A' in printing might just deserve a special treat," grinned Alex.

Sabrina's eyes widened. She looked first at Alex and then back to Nick.

"A treat? Alex…Daddy? What kind of treat?"

"I'm not sure, but I bet we think of something before the day's over."

Mac smiled at Sabrina. She was smart, all right and also cute as a button. Sabrina didn't realize what a heart breaker she was going to be when she grew up. Thank heavens she was only six! Wait until she was a teenager! Nick and Alexandra would be lucky if she didn't have all the boys in her class hanging around.

"Sabrina, did you have fun on the airplane?"

"I loved it, Uncle Mac. No wonder Uncle John likes to fly. Miss Helen let me see a movie and I got pretzels, and juice, too."

"Now that's what I call service," laughed Mac.

"It helps when you own the plane," replied Alex, smiling at her daughter.

"Sabrina? Your Uncle John is still in the hospital. I thought Mom told you."

"She did. I forgot. Is he still there?"

"Yes, honey, he's still there, but he should be able to come home soon."

Alex looked over at Nick. She knew it wasn't going to be easy when John got home. He was used to the services of the hospital, and she wasn't certain how he was going to get around at the ranch. Nick persuaded Maureen to come and see him three days a week, but he still had therapy and counseling in town.

Someone has to drive him back and forth, and someone has to

clean and just be there, at his home. Dr. Martin and Maureen didn't offer any other suggestions to her or to Nicholas. Alex prayed they were making the right choices.

She knew that when she and Nick had to fly back to California, John might feel lost. At least Mac was going to stay with him, for awhile. That would help John—just having someone around to talk to. Alexandra wondered about Kate Walcott. Kate wanted to go and stay at the Ranch to help out. She told Alex she could live in the cottage in back. She seemed so adamant about it, that Alex had almost agreed, but she told Kate she had to speak to Nick first.

Nick Stewart wasn't too sure about Kate. He believed she had so many issues of her own to work out, that perhaps she needed to take care of those first. But, Alexandra made some good points, and she had asked him to reconsider.

"Darling," Alex had said, "it seems like a perfect arrangement. Kate has no place to live. It would not only help her out, but she could cook and clean for John. Since she still has treatments at the hospital, she could drive them into town each day."

Nicholas had given Alex one of "quit playing matchmaker" looks, and he still hadn't given her an answer about Kate.

Kate also asked Alex if she would speak to John about it. Alex hadn't asked, or talked to John yet. She wanted her husband's agreement first.

Nick drove to John's ranch first, so that Alex could put Sabrina's things away. They gave the child a brief tour of the stables, and then the house—and then Sabrina found the cat! Old Yeller had curled up in his favorite place, the chair on the front porch.

"Momma, look! It's a kitty—he doesn't have any tail."

Alexandra laughed. She watched as Old Yeller looked up at the child. Sabrina went toward him and held out her hand. She was taught to stay far enough away, just in case an animal wasn't as friendly as she was. She moved closer, a little at a time and then, scratched the cat's ears. The cat leaned into her little hands and began to purr.

"I'll be," said Mac, who had come from the car.

"She's got him eating out of her hand, already. Just like us, huh?"

Alexandra smiled. Sabrina *was* the apple of her father's eye, all right. Alexandra had come to love the child as if she were her very own. After Nick's first wife died, he and Sabrina were on their own for such a long time. Alex thought it might pose a problem when she married the child's father, but Sabrina had more than welcomed her, and she embraced Alexandra as her own mother. It was a wonderful day for Alex, when she finally called her, "Momma."

"Well, Mac, Old Yeller's pretty lovable too," she chuckled.

The cat had gained at least three extra pounds and was the laziest animal around.

"Sabrina, honey, go and wash your hands and let's go see John, okay? We'll be back here tonight. You can play with the cat then."

"Okay, Momma. Bye, pretty kitty."

The cat looked up at the child and yawned. As she left, he curled back up in his favorite position, napping in the rocking chair.

When the Stewart family and Mac arrived at Saint's hospital, and entered John Cabe's room, there was an instant *celebration!*

"Uncle Johnny!" Sabrina cried out as she ran over and hugged John Cabe.

"Sabrina—wow! This is the best present I could ever ask for."

John let the child settle on his lap, and he leaned down and kissed her forehead. In his mind, he could still see her—fair skin—black curly hair—light blue eyes. He gave her a hug, and felt one of her feet hitting him on his ankle, as she swung them back and forth.

"I bet you've grown a foot since I saw you last."

"I've only grown inches, Uncle Johnny. But, I am a lot smarter!"

John grinned, "I can believe that. How's school?"

Sabrina went on to tell John about her "A" and then told him she had seen his ranch and met his cat.

"You met Old Yeller? How'd you like him?"

"I like him, Uncle John. He's a real smart cat, you know?"

Alexandra and Mac looked at each other. They would never have called the cat "smart." Maybe Sabrina knew something they didn't.

"Oh, I know, Sabrina. He's had to be on his own for a long time before he came to live with me. I can imagine the things that cat has seen and the places he's been."

"He let me pet him. He purred. He knows I won't hurt him."

The child evidently saw "Old Yeller" in a new light. John agreed with Sabrina. Alex punched Nick's side, and smiled as they watched their daughter.

Alex whispered, "John and Sabrina are soul mates, Nick—just like you and me."

Nick Stewart took his wife's hand. He knew what she meant. He had met his soul mate—Alexandra. They were people who were meant to meet, who had an instant bond, and who knew the other person as well as themselves. He had just never thought of an adult and a child being that. He looked at Sabrina and John as they talked about the cat. Alex might just be right.

Just at that moment, Matthew walked into John's room. Sabrina Stewart watched, as the boy headed toward her "Uncle John."

"Hi, John," said Matthew. "Hi, Mr. Stewart, Mr. Timmons—Mrs. Stewart—who's this?"

Matthew stared at Sabrina. She stared back at this "intruder," her dark eyebrows lifting slightly.

"Matthew, this is Sabrina Stewart. She's Nick and Alex's daughter."

"Oh, Hi—" Matthew said.

Sabrina replied, "Hello."

John couldn't tell for certain, but they were awfully quiet. Could they be jealous—of him? He wished he could see them. He bet they were staring each other down right now. Sabrina—only child—Matthew—no parents, but a new friend...

John interrupted the silence.

"Matthew, why don't you show Sabrina the children's wing, where all the toys are—maybe Mac could go with you two?"

"I think that's a great idea," said Alex. "I'll be glad to go along."

"Well, okay—as long as you're there, Momma." Sabrina reluctantly agreed.

Nick and John waited for them to leave. Both of them broke out in laughter when the door closed.

"I think she's jealous, John. You've won my daughter's heart and she doesn't want anyone else sharing it."

John was incredulous.

"Wait until she starts to talk to Matthew. I bet we have a budding romance there."

"Oh boy. Is this what I'm in for when she starts growing up?"

82

"That, and more," grinned John Cabe.

"John, I want to ask you something. Alex has been after me to agree to this. I'm not sure how you'd feel about it. When you get home, Kate Walcott asked if she could take on the job of cooking, cleaning, and driving for you. She has no place to stay. She wants to stay in your cottage, out back.

"If it were anyone else, John, it would seem a perfect solution. Mac will be there with you in the ranch house, and I have Maureen coming to check on you three days a week. Kate would seem to be the answer to a prayer—live-in housekeeper and driver—but..."

"With everything that's happened, you don't know if we're the best people to be together?"

John completed Nick Stewart's exact thought.

"Yes. Alexandra thinks she should be there. I wasn't sure how you'd feel."

Nick watched his friend struggle with this new challenge.

"I think it might be all right, Nick. I don't hate her—not after hearing what happened to her. Did you know she finally reported the rape and the Sheriff told her that it would just be her word against that maniac's? How's that for fair? She can't go home yet. Maybe we could help each other out."

"You think about it, John. I'll let Alex know when you decide. She can talk to Kate Walcott."

John had another decision to make—one that he had not told Nick. He asked Mac to talk to Children's Services to see about Matthew Clark. He wanted to keep Matthew at his ranch for awhile after he returned home. He didn't know how they'd feel about a blind foster father. He asked Mac if both of them could manage to keep Matthew. Mac liked the idea too. He and John had both grown fond of this boy, and he hated to see him go live in a foster home.

Perhaps, if he could let them know that he had a female housekeeper too, they might let him keep the boy. He knew Matthew and Kate were seeing a lot of each other at the hospital, and the boy seemed to be genuinely fond of her.

"I'll let you know before the weekend, Nick."

John knew Alex and Nick were taking Sabrina home in a couple of days. He thought of Maureen and Dr. Martin. He'd hate leaving them. He caught himself wishing it were Maureen staying at his home. At least, he'd see her three days a week for awhile.

Kate's bandages had to be changed today, and she dreaded it. She knew that Dr. Martin would ask her to look in the mirror at the healing process. She hated her face, and kept it covered, even though Dr. Martin had removed most of the bandages.

She wore her hair down over that side of her face, and she had lightly taped a piece of gauze over the right side. She could still see out of the right eye, but her lashes and brow had been burned, and she wasn't certain if they would grow back. She applied makeup to the left side of her face, and felt she looked "halfway normal," if she kept the right side bandaged.

"Kate, how are you today?"

Dr. Martin's cheery greeting made Kate wonder if she would ever feel good about herself again.

"I'm all right. My arm seems a lot better."

"Well, let's see how that face is healing."

He saw a visible cringe from the young woman when he mentioned her face.

"Kate? Is something else bothering you?"

"Dr. Martin? The skin graft—you said that it worked. Is it going to continue to heal? Will I get my eyebrows and lashes back?"

"It is working, Kate. We have to continue with the bandages and the medication. But, why are you continuing to cover up that part of your face that has healed? Does it still hurt?"

"It's not that. It's so red. I just look so ugly."

"Let's take a look at this."

Dr. Martin removed one layer of medicated gauze.

"You were lucky in one way. You only had second-degree burns, Kate. That should not affect the hair follicles, or the tissue. Your lashes and brows should grow back. But, if they don't, there are always fake lashes, and there's makeup. I know you can't use them yet, but you will be able to soon. It's just going to take time."

"I don't know why I feel this way, Dr. Martin. I know I'm really lucky."

Dr. Martin remembered all the things Kate Walcott had been through. It was going to take more than the burns healing. Her *soul* needed healing. She was hurt both physically and emotionally, and her Spirit was struggling.

She had gone through the worst thing a woman could go through, and the police couldn't do anything in resolving the crime that had been committed against her. That violent act against her brought on the suicide attempt. Dealing with her burns weren't as difficult as her guilt over what happened to John Cabe, when he saved her life.

"Kate, I want you to continue coming to counseling. That's going to help. You're way too hard on yourself."

Kate thought about John. He hadn't quite forgiven her, but he was farther along that she was—in forgiving herself. She thought about her stepfather. She would never be able to forgive him—-never! She hated him! She hated the police for doing nothing.

Dr. Martin finished changing the bandages and left the lower part of Kate's face exposed.

"Look, Kate—it's not red today. See? It's pink, but it's coming along."

Kate looked in the mirror. No one would see her anyway. She looked at the small space he left uncovered. It looked as if she might have fallen and skinned herself. It wasn't as red as it had been and she prayed it would heal totally.

"It does look better, Dr. Martin. I'm sorry. I'm just feeling sorry for myself today, I guess."

He smiled down at her.

"Mr. Cabe going to let you go and take care of him?"

Kate looked surprised. How did he know? Had John talked to him about this?

"I'm not sure if anyone has asked him. I talked to Alexandra Stewart. She promised that she'd bring it up to him."

"Perhaps you need to talk to him. Ask him yourself, Kate. You two seem to be at least on 'speaking terms'."

"There's still a coldness there, Dr. Martin. I don't think he completely trusts me yet. He's nice enough, but I never hear a warmth in his voice, except when we talk about Matthew."

Dr. Martin knew what she meant. John Cabe may have said he forgave her, but there was still a lot of resentment hidden there. At least, the two of them were talking to each other.

"Kate? Do you remember when he wouldn't even see you? Now, you talk to him at least once a day. That's promising. Remember when you told us that your best point was not 'patience'?"

Kate laughed. "You can say that again."

"Well, here's two major problems in which you have to be patient—the burns on your face—and John Cabe's friendship and forgiveness."

She knew he was right. Mr. Cabe—John—was more than kind to her. After all that happened, she was grateful he would even speak to her. She thought about Matthew too. She never loved a child before, but she loved Matthew. He made her forget about her own problems. If she could help Matthew, it would help her. He had lost so much more that she had—even more that John Cabe had lost.

"I'll talk to John later today, Dr. Martin. I hope he'll see that I might be a blessing to him, instead of a curse."

"Don't worry, Kate. You can be quite convincing when you want to."

He smiled. He was going to let Maureen keep a watch on them for a few days a week. Later, that wouldn't be necessary. Right now, they were all three so fragile—Kate—John—and most of all, Matthew. Three fragile souls searching for a new life!

Sabrina Stewart showed Matthew how to spin his yo-yo. Her dad had shown her a few tricks and she picked them right up. Matthew watched her hands as she wrapped the string around the toy. She could make it stop in mid-air.

"Wow! That's really good. Can I try it?"

"Sure—here."

She handed him the yo-yo and watched as he clumsily tried to repeat the trick and the string knotted itself inside the toy.

"Oops! Guess I did something wrong—"

"*Boys!*" she thought. "Here, I'll get it undone for you."

He watched as her small fingers found the knot and undid it. She was good.

"I really like your mom and dad," said Matthew.

"Yeah, they're pretty nice, all right. Alex is really my second mom. My first mom died."

Matthew's ears perked up.

"She did?"

"Yes. She was sick a long time."

"I bet you miss her, huh?"

"Yes, but Alex is really nice. I love her and she really makes my dad happy."

"My mom and dad both died. They were in a car crash."

Sabrina took a long look at the boy. She didn't know about his parents. She tried to say something that would make him feel better.

"You must feel really bad. I'm sorry. When my mom died, I cried a lot."

"Yeah, me too. I miss them a lot. They're going to send me to a foster home, you know?"

"No—You could come home with me, Matthew. My mom and dad would take you."

Matthew Clark thought about what life would be like in Nick Stewart's mansion. He bet he'd have ice cream and cake every day. Then, he thought about John and his friend, Kate.

"I really want to stay here, in Arizona. I wish I could live with your Uncle John. I really like him. Or, if Kate had a house, I could stay with her. They both visit me and we talk a lot. That's why I like them."

Sabrina understood why Matthew would want to live with her Uncle John. When he lived in California, before her Dad met Alex, Uncle John would drive her to school when her Dad had to be at work. He was a lot of fun. He played games and sang songs. He acted silly with her. Sabrina thought about it and turned back to Matthew.

"I think you should live with Uncle John. Then, I could see you too. You could even come and visit me in California. Uncle John could fly you there."

"Not anymore. He can't see."

"He will. I know he will. *The angel told me!* Uncle Johnny's going to *see* again."

"What angel?"

"The angel in the hall, downstairs—the one with the red hair. She was really nice. She said not to worry, and that my Uncle John's going to see again."

"I don't believe you. There's no such thing as an angel."

Matthew was indignant.

"There is too!" Sabrina said, as she raised her voice.

Sabrina was adamant about this.

"I saw her. She told me."

Matthew didn't say anything. This dark-haired girl was almost screaming at him. He guessed she really believed she saw an angel. He knew better, but he didn't like it when she yelled.

"Okay, okay, quiet down—so you saw this angel..."

"That's better. Just you remember that, Matthew—when my Uncle Johnny sees you! Meanwhile, you need to go and live with him and help him out."

Sabrina was as certain all of this would work out, as she was that her Dad loved her. There was no question—and no reasoning with her. She simply *BELIEVED!*

Alexandra overheard part of the conversation between the two children. She smiled. Nick's child had more faith than many adults. Alex prayed Sabrina was right about John, and she said a small "thank you" for Sabrina Stewart. This child had been a gift to her, and she loved her like she was her own. She was like Nick in so many ways, and standing her ground was one of them.

Alexandra wondered what her own baby—hers and Nick's—might be like. It had been on her mind a lot recently.

Chapter Nine

Kate used her cane to walk down the hallway to see John. She wasn't surprised to see the door open, and Nicholas Stewart sitting in the room with him. She wanted to speak to John alone—perhaps she should come back later. Nick saw her, and motioned for her to come inside.

"Katherine, please come in."

Alexandra was right. Kate Walcott did look like the picture he had seen downstairs. Without her bandages, Nick would have thought that she posed for the painting!

"I was just going to try and find my wife and daughter. They headed off with Matthew about thirty minutes ago, and still haven't returned."

He was giving her an opportunity to be alone with John—and Kate knew it. She smiled at him, as he pulled out a chair for her. She liked Nicholas Stewart, even though he wasn't too sure about her. Kate couldn't blame him. John was his best friend and look what she had done.

"They're probably in the Children's Unit," Kate said. "I'd love to meet your daughter, Mr. Stewart."

"Please, call me 'Nick'," his voice softened. "I'll see if I can find them. Maybe we'll be back before you leave, Kate."

He smiled at her, and his almost turquoise-blue eyes seemed to look right through her. She knew he must have made his own decision about her.

"Kate?" John Cabe had been silent. "Did you want to see me?"

Nick Stewart excused himself and Kate turned to John.

"I do. I want to ask you something, John."

She swallowed hard, her voice becoming like a whisper.

"Yes?"

"I want to come and live with you, John. I mean—I want to work for you—if you'll have me. I know you need someone to cook and clean. I'd be very good at that."

It took courage. She's got guts. I'll have to give her that.

"I have to think about it, Kate. It might be a solution—for both of us."

Kate's breath caught. He was thinking about it. He didn't say "no" to her. That was good. She didn't know if she dare say anymore, so she was quiet.

"Kate?"

"I'm still here. I was just thinking. I don't know what I would do—if I were in your shoes, John. I just know I want to do this for you, if you'll have me."

"I'm thinking of asking Matthew to come stay with me, for a little while. Would that make a difference to you?"

Kate's heart leaped.

"Matthew? Oh, John. I think that would be wonderful. He needs a father figure and you've been so good to him. Will they let you do it?"

"I'm not sure. I'll have Mac there to help us out. It might make a difference if they knew a woman was going to be there too—to cook and help care for him. Would you be willing to do that?"

There was no question that she would. She loved the boy. It would almost be like having a family again. Kate felt more hopeful than she had in days!

"I would. I'd love helping you take care of him, John. You know, we've really gotten to be friends, Matthew and I."

"I know. He talks about you a lot."

John Cabe made up his mind.

"I'd like having you there, Kate. It would make things easier...if you're sure?"

Kate Walcott couldn't resist. She went over to John's chair and hugged him—right there in his hospital room. John was a little stunned, but he smiled at her enthusiasm.

"Thank you, John—I promise you won't regret it. Thank you, so much!"

She was still clinging to his neck, when she realized what she was doing. She stepped back.

"I'm sorry. I was just so thrilled," she stammered.

"It's okay, Kate."

He smiled at her, thinking it wasn't so bad—that hug.

"I'm glad you want the job that much," he grinned.

Kate Walcott didn't consider it a job, as much as her own *redemption!*

Nick Stewart ran into Dr. Martin on his way to find Alex and Sabrina.

"Good day, Nicholas. How are you?"

"Dr. Martin, I'm fine. How are things going?"

"I think your daughter knows, Nicholas. You might want to ask her." Dr. Martin smiled. "She's a precious child, Nick. She has more belief than most adults. It's true, you know?"

"What's that Doc?"

"A little child shall lead them."

Nick was silent for a moment. It was the way Dr. Martin said it that made Nick believe that both Sabrina and Matthew were very important pieces in this puzzle of souls.

"I believe that," Nick replied. "Children are the innocence we all wish for. We stand in awe of them, I think, wishing we could have it back."

Dr. Martin smiled at Nicholas Stewart. This man had learned so much in the past few months. It was good to have him around. He would miss Nick and his family when they returned to California. But—of course—they would meet again. Nick and Alexandra Stewart were about to receive a very special blessing. They just didn't know it, yet.

"I just saw your daughter and your lovely wife with Matthew Clark. They're in the children's wing, Nick. Mr. Timmons was there, but I believe he went to the coffee shop."

"Thanks, Doc. I was just on my way there. I hope to see you before we fly back to California. If I don't, I want to say 'thank you' for giving my life back to me—back then. I'll be praying for John and Kate, and especially for Matthew."

"They're going to be fine, Nicholas. I feel it."

Dr. Martin headed toward his office, while Nick stood there a moment, watching him. Nick would never forget what had happened to him and Alex, what was still happening for John and Kate—and for Matthew. He turned and headed to the Children's Unit.

Alexandra watched Matthew and Sabrina play. Matthew reminded her of Nicholas. He let Sabrina rant and rave for a little while and then, he ended up calming her down, or ignoring her, until she did it his way. She grinned at both of them. They were both about the same size and age. Matthew must be about six to seven years old. He was smart. He was working on his puzzles and math, and he loved those airplanes! Sabrina complimented him as she worked on her painting and artwork. She chattered away, while he listened…like Nicholas did for Alex.

Alex thought that it was too bad Sabrina didn't have a brother. She was enjoying playing with Matthew. Maybe John could bring him to California to visit, if things worked out, and if he got to keep him. She never imagined John wanting a child, before the accident. Now, he seemed perfect for it—and his ranch was a home that Matthew needed.

She prayed John would recover, so that he could see this wonderful child—and Kate. Alex liked Kate. She knew Nick didn't quite trust her yet, but she sensed that he would—sometime soon.

As if reading her thoughts, her husband walked in behind her, put his arm around her waist and kissed the side of her neck, and then her cheek.

"Penny for your thoughts," he whispered.

Alex pointed to the two children, who were playing quietly for a change. Nick watched them, his chin resting on top of Alexandra's head.

"Matthew reminds me of you, Nicholas. He's so gentle, and he listens to Sabrina. She just chatters on and on—and he listens. You do that, Love. You know? I was kind of wishing he could come and visit us. They seem to be getting along so well."

"You kind of like him, huh?"

"Yes. I hope Johnny gets to keep him. They need each other, Nick."

"I know. Things will work out, Alex. They have to."

Alexandra continued, "I was also thinking that Sabrina might be lonely."

She stopped. What she was thinking surprised even her. In her mind, she had just envisioned another child—her child. *How selfish of me!* She had so much—Nick, Sabrina—still, Alexandra had thought so much about this lately. She didn't even want to say it out loud. The truth was, she wanted to have another child—Nick's child—their child.

"Lonely? I've never thought of Sabrina as being lonely," he said. "She has so many friends, Alex."

Alexandra realized that she was avoiding telling Nick what she was thinking. This wasn't an easy subject, and this wasn't the time, or the place. She squeezed his hand.

"You're probably right. I'm just making more of this because of the situation with Matthew. I guess I better go and get John. It doesn't look like these two want to leave. He needs to come down here."

"He's talking to Kate Walcott. That's why I left. I think he's going to ask her to stay with him."

"Oh, Nick! I think that's a good thing. I hope they can work it out."

She turned to face him, looked up and kissed him. Nick Stewart wasn't certain, but he thought his wife had something on her mind that she hadn't yet told him.

After Kate left, John buzzed for Maureen. He could hear her approaching by the usual swish that her skirt made. He smiled as he thought of how she looked to him, in his mind.

"John Cabe! I was beginning to think you were ignoring me," she said.

"Maureen, you know I'd never do that. I just wanted to tell you I'm glad you're going to visit me at my home. I didn't think I'd ever say it, but I'm going to miss this place.

"I guess I'm a little scared to go home. It's going to be so different—finding out where everything is again—not being able to ring or buzz someone when I need something. I don't know if I'm ready."

"John, you'll be able to hold that old cat of yours, again. Mr. Timmons will be there with you. I'll make certain that I get out there the very first day. Don't worry. You are going to be fine. I just know that you're going to see again. Trust me. Do you believe me, John?"

John smiled. They had a "sort of" pact. He had to believe her and she couldn't lie to him.

"I believe," he said.

"Good."

"Kate Walcott's going to come to the ranch, Maureen. I wanted to tell you that I agreed to it. She's going to cook for Mac and for me. She said she'd clean too. That'll help, I think."

"That's great, John. See? I told you things would work out for the two of you."

"I haven't heard from Children's Services yet about Matthew. I asked to take him home with me."

"I know. Don't worry. They'll let you take him for a visit, at least. Then, they're going to see how good you and Kate are with him. He's already so bonded to both of you."

"I hope you're right, Maureen. I don't know if he needs me more, or if I need him. I really love that child."

Maureen smiled. They all need each other—silly humans—everyone needs someone—

Alexandra Stewart walked into John's room at that moment and she smiled at his nurse. It was the first time that Alex had met Maureen McConnell in person. She introduced herself and stared. She had heard John and Nick's description of Maureen, but she saw, instead, a middle-aged woman with reddish-brown hair. She looked nothing like Kate, or the picture of the Saint, and not much like John's description of her. Alex thought about what Dr. Martin had told her, and kept quiet.

Kate Walcott was beautiful, even with her scars. She was the person that John had described when he told Nicholas what Maureen looked like. Maureen was close to being "plain" in appearance, next to Kate. Still, there was a softness to her and a glow that seemed to surround her. Alexandra found her voice was pleasant—songlike.

"I'm so happy to meet you, Mrs. Stewart. I've heard so many good things about you from this one here."

She had an Irish accent. That was unmistakable. Alex smiled back at her.

"Thank you, Maureen. I've heard only good things about you, too."

Alex turned to John.

"Johnny, if you're going to visit Sabrina and Matthew, you're going to have to come to the children's wing. They're nowhere close to being ready to quit their games and playtime. They've gotten to be very good friends."

"See, I told Nick that. I bet Sabrina has Matthew twisted around her little finger by now. I could tell that when they met. I'll be along, if you'll give me a push, Alex."

"That would be my pleasure, Sir."

She glanced back where Maureen McConnell stood smiling at them.

"Nice meeting you finally, Maureen."

Maureen walked over to Alexandra, touched her shoulder, and said something strange.

"The Lord's just blessed you, Mrs. Stewart, and it's the thing you want the most."

Alexandra Stewart didn't know what Maureen meant. She tucked the thought away, and pushed John toward the children's wing. She was thinking about what Maureen had just told her, when John Cabe asked her a question that she wasn't prepared for either.

"Alex, what is it? There's something wrong, isn't there?"

"What makes you think that?"

"I don't know, Beautiful. I guess I just know you. Tell me."

She couldn't tell if John sensed something about what Maureen just said, or if he had caught her mood. Alex had so many moods lately! She was either crying or laughing—so sad at times, she couldn't get out of her dark places, or so happy, she was on the ceiling.

Either way, she wasn't prepared to tell John that she wanted a baby, and, she couldn't tell him that she believed Maureen McConnell was really an angel!

Alex stuttered, "I—I don't know what you're talking about. I'm fine. I was just thinking that maybe Matthew could visit us when you get him. I think Sabrina needs—company."

"Sure. That's a great idea, but it's not what you're thinking about, Alexandra."

"You're right. You know me too well, John Cabe. I just think that Nicholas has to be the first person I talk to. I was just thinking how much I'd love it if I—if we..."

She was almost in tears again, and didn't have the slightest idea why.

"You feel Okay, Alex?"

"Certainly. I just get these strange moods, lately. I don't know what's wrong with me. I'm either up in the clouds or crying my eyes out!"

"Alexandra, are you pregnant?"

She was astonished at John Cabe. He didn't know how close he was to guessing what she wanted more than anything in the world. She wasn't pregnant, though, not yet.

"No, of course not—not that it wouldn't be wonderful—having a baby—Nick's baby—with me."

John grinned and asked her to please stop pushing the wheelchair.

"Come around here, Alex—in front of me."

She walked around and knelt in front of John. She had an overwhelming urge to cry even harder, and she did. John reached out for her hand.

"Do you want a child, Alexandra Stewart? There's nothing more that Nick would want than to be able to give you that gift. You think that he doesn't want another baby? You probably think you're being selfish, don't you? You don't know your husband, if you think that, Alex. Sabrina would love a little brother or sister—now, you take Nick Stewart somewhere—back to my ranch if you have to—you sit down and you tell him. You hear me, Beautiful?"

Alex rose, leaned over and hugged John.

"You're my best friend, Johnny Cabe. You know me better than anyone." She was crying. "I love you, John."

"I know. All the women say that."

His eyes were moist. She was *his* best friend too—they shared a bond that would never be broken.

Alexandra pushed John into the children's unit where Nick, Sabrina and Matthew were waiting. John suggested that Sabrina and Matthew stay with him, and they could have dinner together. Smiling, he told Nick that he needed his cell phone, and that it was back at his ranch. He asked Nicholas if he'd mind going and picking it up. Alex smiled. She knew what he was doing for her. She squeezed John's hand, and told Nick that she'd ride back to John's ranch with him — to pick up his phone.

Mac had gone into town and to the diner. He bought a bucket of fried chicken and biscuits. He thought the kids and John would like that. He also ordered two side orders of French Fries and coleslaw, and then stopped at the grocery and picked up some ice cream. He was ready to give them a party — a real picnic!

When he arrived at the hospital, both children were already back in John's room and were working on one of Matthew's model airplanes. John was telling them a story about an airliner.

"Hey, anyone in here ready for fried chicken?" Mac shouted as he entered.

"Boy, that sounds good! You must have read our minds, Mac," John answered.

"He has ice cream, too, Uncle Johnny," squealed Sabrina.

"It sure smells good, Mac," Matthew chimed in.

"Decided we'd have a party," said Mac. "Where are Nick and Alex?"

"I think they're probably having their own *party*," grinned John Cabe.

Mac looked over at John, shrugged, and passed out the food.

Alexandra made some coffee, while Nick searched for John's cell phone.

"I don't understand why he needs this tonight," he said. "I haven't the slightest idea where it could be, Alex."

"I'll find it later, Love. Come and sit down with me. I'm making some coffee, and, I need to talk to you."

They were alone, but it wasn't how she would have planned it. She wanted soft music, and candles, and everything — *just perfect*. Instead, she picked up Old Yeller from the sofa and put him on her lap. She stroked his head, as Nick sat down beside them, taking her hand.

"What is it, Alexandra? Is something wrong?"

"No, darling. I just don't know how to say what I want to say to you."

He squeezed her hand, "Just tell me, Alex. You know you can tell me anything."

Nick sensed that she had wanted to speak to him earlier, but couldn't. He thought of all the things that had happened since they arrived in Clarksville and at Saint's Hospital. It must be about John or Kate, or…suddenly, he was getting a little anxious when she didn't say *anything*. He moved closer to his wife.

"I—I love you so much, Nicholas," she said.

"I love you too, Alex."

"I want a child, Nick."

It wasn't how she wanted to phrase it. When it came out, it sounded harsh, even to her—demanding! It was all wrong!

"Do you mean Matthew? You want us to keep Matthew?"

"No! I mean—our child—I want your…"

She burst into tears again.

"What's wrong with me?" she asked, as she got up to find a tissue, "I can't go two minutes without crying!"

Nick Stewart wasn't certain that he heard what he *thought* he heard.

"Alex?"

He got up and tried to put his arms around her, but she wouldn't let him comfort her and shrugged him away. She was almost sobbing now. If he heard her right—if he heard what he thought he heard—

"Alexandra? Did you just tell me you want *us* to have a child?"

Her tears had become a flood now and she couldn't stop them. *What if he said "no"? But, why would he say "no"?* She wasn't making any sense, and she knew it. She gulped, and tried to continue.

"John—Johnny told me I just needed to go ahead, rush right in, and tell you. I want our very own baby, Nicholas. I love Sabrina so much, Nicholas, but I want…"

She looked away from him. It did sound selfish! She had so many blessings.

He caught her by her shoulders before she turned away, again. Turning her toward him, he pulled her so tight to him, she couldn't move.

"Oh, Alexandra. Oh, Babe, I love you so much."

He was laughing.

"Are you laughing at me?"

Her tears stopped. Indignation was getting ready to replace them! She was at the edge of being paranoid—worst of all, she knew it.

"Of course, I'm not laughing at you. I'm laughing because I'm relieved. I thought you wanted to tell me something *terrible,* but instead, it's the most wonderful thing in the world! Don't you know that Alex? I love you more than life, itself. Of course, I want that."

He held her close and then leaned down, brushed her hair away from her face, and then kissed away her tears, one by one.

Alexandra trembled.

He finally found her mouth, and kissed her gently. When she looked up at him, he looked right through her, and into her soul, with those wonderful turquoise-blue eyes. Why had she ever doubted?

"This wasn't the way I planned to tell you, Nick. I wanted candles and music."

"We have them," he answered. "I hear the music in your heart, and I can imagine the candlelight. Just close your eyes, Alexandra. Lean on me—and listen."

He pulled her even closer. She closed her eyes and she heard the music. She saw the candlelight.

Nick and Alexandra Stewart were very late returning to the hospital that evening.

Chapter Ten

When the Stewarts later returned to the hospital, they found Sabrina asleep in John's hospital bed. John was sitting in his chair, and Mac was watching both of them, almost dozing off too.

"Now, this is sad," Alexandra chuckled.

"Sorry we're late, John," Nick said to his friend. "I never did find that cell phone of yours."

John Cabe smiled, "That's okay, Buddy. We had a good time, here. Mac bought us a real picnic. I think that we partied your girl and Matthew out, though. She's been asleep about fifteen minutes."

Alex was already removing Sabrina's shoes, and she motioned for Nick to carry her out to the car. Mac yawned, got up, and stretched.

"I think I'm ready to hit the hay, too. I'll meet you out in the car, Alex."

"Okay. I'll be right there."

She watched, as Mac left with Nicholas and Sabrina.

"Well?" asked John.

"It was wonderful. I can't tell you how wonderful, but I can thank you for your help. How did you know, Johnny?"

"Maybe, it's because I lost my sight—you know what they say about the other senses getting sharper."

He grinned, and Alex knew he was joking with her. But, she, on the other hand, was very serious when she answered him.

"No, I know it's not that, John. It's more. It has something to do with this place, I think. But, most of all, you know me, John Cabe. You always have. You know Nicholas too. What a friend you've been to us. You'll never know how much we appreciate you—how much we love you."

John wasn't prepared to hear this. He was moved by what she said to him. He reached for her hand.

"Hey, Beautiful—that goes both ways, you know?"

"I do know. I have to go now, but I'll see you first thing tomorrow."

Alex Stewart kneeled down and gave him a kiss on his forehead, then got up quickly to leave. Instead, she grew dizzy and, all of a sudden, the room began to spin—round and round. She felt the wave of nausea hit her. The room started to fade, then grew dark. Alex fainted, sliding right past John's lap—and onto the floor.

"Alexandra! What the...?"

John felt her as she fell across his lap and as she slid past him, further down. He tried to catch her, but it was so unexpected. He yelled for a nurse—anyone to help!

Alex woke up in a hospital bed, with Nick, Mac, and Sabrina all watching her from its side.

"What happened?" she asked.

"You passed out cold, kid," Mac replied.

"Alex, are you all right?" Nick asked her.

Nicholas was holding onto her hand, and looking very worried. Alexandra reached for his face.

"I'm fine, I think. I was just talking to John and when I got up to leave, I felt sick—then, everything just blacked out."

"Momma, are you going to be okay?" asked Sabrina, who squeezed under her dad's arm and grabbed Alexandra's other hand.

"Oh, darling—I'll be fine. I just need to rest a minute."

"Mac, would you take Sabrina outside? I need to talk to Alexandra."

"Sure, Nick. Come on, young lady. Let's go get something to drink, until Dr. Martin gets back. He's going to let us know what's going on with your Mom, okay?"

"And, you'll tell me? Daddy, will you tell me?"

Nicholas leaned down, and kissed his daughter.

"I'll tell you everything, Sabrina, as soon as I know something."

"Nick, I've never fainted—I promise. I would have told you. I have had some nausea, but mostly, it's just been a little lightheadedness—and these crazy mood swings. I cry at the drop of a hat. It's nothing serious. It can't be—not now."

She suddenly felt like crying, but she couldn't, not in front of him. He looked so worried, as it was.

"Dr Martin wants to run some tests. He wants you to stay here tonight, Alex."

"Nick, no! Not tonight."

Dr. Anthony Martin came strolling into the room. He didn't look worried. He had a large smile on his face.

"Dr. Martin, do you know anything?" asked Nick.

"Nicholas—Alexandra—I want to take a little blood, just to be sure about something. Nick, Do you mind waiting outside, for just a minute?"

He did mind. Nick Stewart didn't want to leave her, not even with Dr. Martin—not for one moment, but he thought about it. Dr. Martin didn't look concerned. Maybe it was nothing, after all.

"I'll be just outside, darling."

He squeezed her hand and left the room.

"What is it, Dr. Martin?"

Alex was worried too. She had been so happy when she returned from the ranch. She said a little prayer, while Dr. Martin listened to her pulse and checked her heart rate.

"Alexandra, I think you may be pregnant. I just want to make sure. But, I think it's safe for me to tell you that otherwise, you seem perfectly healthy."

"Pregnant? But, I—we just decided—just tonight."

She was flabbergasted.

"You forget. God is the One who makes *some* decisions. He has a sense of humor, Alex. He may have just timed this, when you and Nicholas 'decided' it was time. You rest. I'll be right back. This won't take long. Then, we'll know for certain."

He left the room, leaving Nick, Mac and Sabrina outside in the hallway. Alex took a deep breath. Suddenly, it all made sense—her nausea—the dizziness—even the mood swings! Her hormones must be doing flip-flops! She remembered what Dr. Martin and Maureen had told her—*a gift to be entrusted to her—a blessing—something she wanted more than anything—could it be?*

Could it be possible she was already expecting a child when they told her this? Could it be they knew it was hers and Nick's child? How could they have known? She could barely wait for Dr. Martin to return!

Anthony Martin liked this day! It was a good day! He came from the lab, and turned down the hallway, back to Alex Stewart's room. He opened her door, and just grinned at her, and then gave her a nod. She tried to get up from the bed to move toward him, almost falling back into it. She was still dizzy. He laughed and went over to help her up. That's when Alexandra threw her arms around Dr. Martin and hugged him.

"Oh, thank you! Thank you God! Thank you, Dr. Martin!"

Nicholas Stewart heard the small commotion, and went into his wife's room. He wasn't prepared for what he saw—his wife, hugging the doctor that he believed to be an angel!

"Oh, Nicholas. It's so wonderful! I can hardly believe it."

"Alexandra? Is she all right, Dr. Martin?"

Nick went to her side and she clung to him, tighter than ever.

"She's just fine, Nicholas."

"I'm pregnant, Nick," smiled Alexandra, "I'm already pregnant! We're going to have a child."

"What? But—how? Well, I guess I know how, but we just talked about it."

Nick wasn't used to being speechless, but he was. He leaned down and kissed his wife. He had tears in his eyes, and both of them were laughing and crying at the same time. He knew exactly how Alex felt with the mood swings that she had told him about.

"I can't imagine any two people who are more deserving than the two of you. Congratulations, Nicholas—Alexandra."

Dr. Anthony Martin left the room, telling Alex that she could go home tonight if she wanted to.

"Where's Sabrina? We have to tell her, and Johnny and Mac."

"Calm down—I don't know if it's good for you. Oh, Alex, I cannot believe this! I'm so happy. Are you happy? Of course, you are!"

Alex watched her husband. He was talking a mile a minute. She had to laugh. She was bubbling over, herself. As she tried to stand up again, she fell—right into his arms!

John Cabe had stayed in his room, waiting to hear some news about his friend. He paced the floor. Alex had to be all right. He heard a noise, and then heard the entire group coming back to his room. He could hear Sabrina laughing and talking to her mother. He heard Mac saying how wonderful this was. *What was going on?*

It was Alex he heard coming into his room, first. He could hear her telling the rest of them to wait outside.

"Hey, Beautiful. What's going on? Are you all right?"

"I just wanted to be the one to tell you, John. I'm fine—more than fine. Johnny, I'm pregnant!"

"What?"

He remembered asking her earlier if she was, but she said no.

"I just didn't know it. I didn't realize what was going on. I've been so busy lately, and these symptoms have been going on over a month now. John—darling John—I'm having a baby. Nick and I are having our baby."

She was holding his hands, and he didn't know what to say. He got up from his chair, leaned down, and kissed her—his best friend, this wonderful lady. He had chills. It was the best news they had in days.

Then, Nick, Mac, and Sabrina came into the room. There was so much excitement that any thought of bedtime, or sleeping, vanished. Mac left to go get soft drinks, and something else for all of them to snack on. They "had" to have a cake, he told them. The night turned into a celebration. They were celebrating a new life—and it was pure joy!!

Chapter Eleven

The weekend passed too soon for all of them. It was time for Nick and Alex to fly home with Sabrina. John and Mac said goodbye to them and before they left, Alex went to visit with Kate, Maureen and Dr. Martin. Nick promised John that they would be back a month from today—sooner if he needed them.

John was sorry to see the Stewarts leave, but he was now one day closer to going home to his ranch. Tomorrow, he and Kate Walcott would begin their own new journey. Later in the week, he would find out from Children's Services about Matthew. Until then, at least the Social Worker was going to allow Matthew to visit them. The day after tomorrow, they could pick up Matthew and take him back to the ranch with them—even if it was just for the week.

"I'll go back to the ranch and get your jeans and a shirt to wear home," said Mac. "It'll be good to get you back home, John. You'll see. Everything's going to work out for the good."

John wasn't so sure. He still had some doubts in the back of his mind, and they included Katherine Walcott and Matthew Clark.

The next morning, Kate climbed up into the back seat of John Cabe's jeep. Mac was driving them back to the ranch today. She didn't know why she was so nervous. Tomorrow, Matthew would join them.

It will be easier for him, then, she thought, as she stared up front at John.

She leaned back against the leather seat and watched the countryside slide by. It was strange. She would have guessed that all of Arizona would be nothing but desert, but up here, there were hills and greenery that she hadn't expected. As Mac turned from the Interstate onto the two-lane highway, Kate gasped.

"My God!" she exclaimed, partially under her breath.

They were passing by the same exact spot where the "accident" had happened.

Accident? It was no accident. I tried to run the car off the road and commit suicide!

If she were to drive John Cabe to the hospital each day, as she had agreed, she would have to pass this horrible reminder daily! She didn't know if she could handle it.

"Kate?"

John turned in his seat to face her. He sensed something was wrong.

"Are you all right, back there?"

"Sure. I'm okay."

Kate wasn't too good at disguising what she felt, but she tried to sound as if she were in a good mood.

John didn't know exactly where they were, but he remembered where the wreck had taken place.

Oh, boy, we must be close to the crash site. This has to be hard for her.

John was glad he couldn't see it—or Kate's reaction to what she saw. He turned in his seat to talk to her. Perhaps, he could do something to help.

"Kate? I don't remember. Did you say you liked animals?"

Kate was surprised by the question. She remembered telling him.

"Sure. I look forward going riding with Matthew, when he gets here."

"No. I mean pets. Do you have any?"

"I never had any. I always thought I might like to have a dog, but my parents moved around a lot when I was younger."

She thought of her real father. He had a job as an engineer that took them all over the world. Kate had seen a lot of countries, but that was a long time ago. She remembered that she and her mother were happy, back then.

"Well, you have to meet John's cat!" chimed in Mac.

"Oh, the famous cat," she grinned.

John wasn't sure of her reaction, but he was determined to make 'Old Yeller' sound attractive to her now.

"Old Yeller is quite a cat, Kate. He came to me right out of the blue and he's managed to make himself at home—right on my front porch."

He smiled when he thought about the cat.

Kate saw the smile. The animal must be more important to him than he said.

"That's quite some name," she laughed. "Where'd you think that up?"

"Remember the movie—the one about the dog? It was a long time ago. You would have been just a child. You may be too young to remember it."

"I remember it. I think my parents rented it. In case you need to know, I'm almost twenty-eight years old. I have a birthday coming up—next month."

"Oh, a birthday, huh?"

"It's nothing. I shouldn't have mentioned it, but it's on my job application."

"I counted on Alex Stewart to read that to me," he laughed, "I guess she skipped that part."

John remembered thinking she was younger. She looked young to him when she passed him in her car. She was only a few years younger than he was.

"I'll be glad to get to the ranch. How much farther, Mac?"

"We're almost there—about another five minutes."

John felt his muscles tighten up. Soon, he would be home and he couldn't help wondering what he was going to do, once he got there.

Mac felt sorry for the woman. He didn't know why he had such compassion for her. She had blinded his friend, but she seemed so "lost" to him. John told Mac some of her story. Mac didn't know how she had made it this far, at times. And John—his John—this just has to work out for him. Mac said a prayer for both John and Kate, as he drove up the driveway to the ranch house.

Kate let John hold onto her arm as he went up the front porch steps. He had never noticed before. There were three steps. He was finally on his own front porch! He felt for the swing and then the rocker. As he reached down, a soft ball of fur stretched, lifted his head and yawned at the two people who were peering down at him.

"This must be Old Yeller," laughed Kate. "He's looking right at you, John. He's glad you're home."

John found the cat's ears, and scratched behind them. He could hear the animal purring.

"Hi there, fellow. It's been awhile, hasn't it?"

As he picked the cat up, he noticed how much heavier he felt.

"They must have fed you pretty good. You weigh a ton!"

"Come on, John. Let's go inside. Kate, come into the ranch house first. I want to show you where John and I will be staying. Then, I'll take you around back to the cottage where you'll be living."

Mac went to get the luggage, while Kate showed John where a chair was. He sat down, holding onto the cat, and trying to relax.

"Kate, go ahead and look around. You need to know where everything is."

Kate took a look at her surroundings. It was nice. It was more comfortable than she imagined. She walked from the living room into the kitchen and opened the cupboard doors.

"Mac must have stocked up," she said to John.

When she walked to the refrigerator, the cat jumped off John's lap and followed her.

"Oh, Yeller, you hungry? John, where's his food? I think he wants something to eat."

"It used to be in that right hand cabinet, the top one, unless Mac stored something else in there."

"I see it. It's still in the cabinet, right where you said."

Kate found the bowl that the cat used, and filled it with some dry food. Yeller decided that she could stay—she had fed him.

"I need some help here," called Mac.

Kate went to the door, and opened it for him. He was loaded down with John's suitcases, and his meds. He was also juggling Kate's.

"Thanks," he laughed. "Are you finding everything?"

"Yes. I'll fix supper later. You can show me where everything in the kitchen is, if I can't find it."

John was noticeably quiet. Kate and Mac looked at each other. They both knew it must be difficult. He had lived here alone. Now, there were two more people living in his house.

"Mac, why don't you show me where the cottage is? I can go and put my things away, and give you and John some time alone. I'll be back in a couple of hours to begin dinner."

Mac knew she was giving John a chance to breathe. He smiled at her, grabbed her hand, and then nodded. He mouthed a silent "thank you."

Mac gave Kate her keys, and showed her where the cottage was. He started to go with her, but she told him she would be fine.

"You need to stay with him," she whispered to him.

When Kate left, John got up, and felt his way around his home. He realized that no one had moved anything. He remembered most of the room. Mac asked him if he could help, but John waved him away.

"I'll put on some coffee, John."

"Fine, Mac. That sounds good. I just want to remember where everything is."

Mac didn't know what to say. He went to the kitchen and put on a pot of coffee. It was going to take time. Mac wondered when Maureen would be here. She might know what to say to John.

Kate Walcott opened the cottage door and put her suitcase inside. She was surprised once more. The cottage was not like the ranch house at all. It was smaller, but it had bright curtains in the small kitchen and someone had put fresh flowers on the table. Even the sofa and chair were in a matching bright chintz cover. They had a yellow background with blue cornflowers.

The cottage was charming! She walked into the bedroom. There must have once been a woman who lived or stayed here at one time, she thought. The bed had a handmade quilt on top of it, with a white lace bed skirt. The dresser and chest of drawers appeared to be old and were very expensive antiques.

"Someone who lived here was very loved," she mused.

Kate couldn't begin to explain the presence of love that surrounded her there. She walked into the bath, already knowing what it would look like.

"A claw footed tub," she smiled. "I always wanted one of these."

She didn't notice the white-haired woman who had walked into the cottage behind her and followed her into the bath.

"Dear?" the woman said.

Kate jumped. She didn't know anyone had followed her inside. She must have left the door open.

"Oh, I'm sorry. I didn't mean to frighten you. I'm Mrs. Simpson, Mr. Cabe's neighbor. I've been feeding his cat while he's been away."

Kate stared at the woman. She might be her own grandmother. She must be checking to see who's out here, poking around.

"Hello. I'm Katherine...Kate Walcott. I'm Mr. Cabe's new housekeeper. We just arrived home. I'll be living out here."

"I'm happy to meet you. I brought this over, for supper."

Mrs. Simpson had a warm homemade apple pie in her hands.

"Oh, you must go to Mr. Cabe's house. He will love meeting you."

"I really don't want to disturb him, today, my dear. I know he must be dealing with other things right now. Just tell him I dropped this off. I'll meet him later in the week, when he's more used to..."

The woman was considerate, thought Kate. She took the pie from her and thanked her.

"Mrs. Simpson, may I ask you something?"

"Anything, dear. How can I help?"

"Who used to live here? I mean, out here, in this cottage?"

Ruth Simpson smiled. She looked at the woman's beautiful auburn hair and her face that had a bandage on one side. *So, this was the girl—she was finally back home!*

Mrs. Simpson told Kate that a management company took over the place before Mr. Cabe bought it, but she remembered a young couple that lived in the cottage almost thirty years ago.

"They were very much in love," she continued. "When they first moved here, they were newlyweds. They had an infant, a little girl. She was about two years old when they moved away. There were a few renters after that, but the cottage, for the most part, has remained the same as it was when they lived in it."

"But everything is in such good shape. It looks as if they just moved out."

"Yes, It's difficult to explain, but they moved almost twenty-six years ago. Of course, Mr. Cabe left everything in here the same. The new ranch house was being built just after the couple moved. I guess they started it, but the husband's work forced them to move before it was completed."

"So, they never saw the new house completed?" asked Kate.

"No, just the framing of it. The management company took over and the couple must have had them complete it, because they rented out the larger house. I think they kept it for a long time, until they finally sold it to John Cabe. I heard that the man died. His wife checked out the rental once or twice, but no one ever lived in the cottage, except for guests, until now."

Kate watched the woman touch the flowers that were on the kitchen table.

"Looks like someone welcomed you," she said.

"It must have been Mr. Timmons—Mac," Kate answered.

"Oh, yes, I've met him. He's such a nice man. He really loves Mr. Cabe."

"Yes, he does."

"Well, I must run. It's been nice talking to you Kate. Come visit me sometime. I'm just down the road. Welcome home."

Kate had a sudden burst of brightness in her soul when Mrs. Simpson said that.

Welcome home...

Kate said it over in her mind.

The cottage felt like "home" to her, and she couldn't explain why.

It was about one hour before dinnertime. Kate walked back to John's ranch house, carrying the apple pie that Ruth Simpson had left them. She knocked on the back door and waited until Mac yelled for her to "Come in." She entered through the screened in back porch, and then walked into the kitchen.

"Kate, you don't have to knock," said Mac. "Just come on in."

"I come bearing gifts," she said. "Look what our neighbor just left us."

Kate walked over to where John Cabe sat and put the pie directly under his nose.

"Apple pie?" he asked, smiling.

"You've got that right, John, and it looks delicious. Ruth Simpson brought it over. She welcomes you home—didn't want to disturb you yet, so she left it with me."

"That's really nice," said Mac. "They're a nice couple. They've sure been feeding this cat a lot of food. Look at him—he's gotten fat, just since I've been here."

John rubbed Old Yeller's tummy. He just rolled over and purred. Kate laughed at them.

"John, you do have one spoiled pet, there."

She went into the kitchen and turned on the oven, then washed some potatoes and put them in to bake.

"Dinner should be ready in about an hour. I thought I'd fix the pork chops I saw in the frig—and a salad, if that's all right—and the baked potatoes. Tomorrow, I'll plan a little better—especially with Matthew's coming here."

John heard the excitement in her voice. Kate was going to be glad about Matthew, and so was he. He was relieved she felt that way.

"The meal sounds good, Kate," replied John, "especially since all we've had recently is hospital food."

Kate found she wasn't certain if she was supposed to eat with them, or not. Maybe she was just supposed to cook. She could always take a tray back over to her cottage, but then she had to clean up after the meal. It was a little awkward. They hadn't discussed any rules that she was to follow. There was only one way to find out.

"Uh, John? Do you want me to stay for dinner, or let you guys eat alone and then come back?"

John couldn't believe he hadn't made things clearer for her.

"Oh, Kate, I'm sorry. I meant to give you some kind of schedule. Of course, you'll eat with us. You're 'family' now. Forgive me for not clarifying that. I'll go over some things with you after dinner."

He had made her sound welcome, and he called her 'family'! She could hardly believe it. She glanced over at him, as she fixed the salad. Mac had given him a headset so that he could listen to the CD player, but she noticed he wasn't using it.

"What kind of music do you like, John?" she asked.

John heard the question, but he was listening to Kate's voice. It was nice. It was similar to Maureen's—without the Irish accent. It was kind of nice having her around.

"Oh, I like a little of everything, except some of those rap songs, or the hard rock. I just don't consider them music. I guess I'm too old fashioned. I like jazz—some country tunes—and some of the old standard songs."

Kate asked if he'd turn the CD player on, so they could all hear it. Music would make it nicer. Mac had gone outside on the front porch swing, and John turned on the music. He got up, and began to walk over to one of the bar stools, where the kitchen divider was. Kate watched as he made his way, holding onto chairs and some of the other furniture. He moved slowly toward her.

She watched as he made it, found a stool, and sat down close to where she was working. She knew it was a triumph for him, but neither of them said anything. John just continued the conversation, as if nothing had happened. Inside, Kate cheered for him!

"Kate, I'm sorry about the schedule. I haven't been very thoughtful. How's the cottage? Do you need anything?"

"No. Nothing—the cottage is perfect. In fact, I've never seen a house that I liked better in a long time. I must remember to thank Mac for the flowers. They were waiting on the kitchen table. They were beautiful."

John smiled, "I'm glad you liked them. I have to admit it. *I* ordered them before I left the hospital."

She was not only surprised, but also somewhat embarrassed. John had been the one who gave her the flowers.

"Oh, I just thought you were too busy, John. Thank you. They're lovely. I never got flowers from anyone before."

John couldn't believe that. She was still young—pretty from what he remembered, and from when he touched her face. No one had ever sent her flowers?

"I can't believe that, Kate. Some man sure messed up. You deserve flowers."

He found himself saying something to her that he wished he hadn't. He'd scare her away, if he weren't careful. After what she'd been through, she must hate men.

"No, John, it's true. You're the first one. I guess no one ever thought that I might like that. Actually, at one time, I was really independent. I've always worked hard, and I never took 'no' for an answer—even from a man. Sometimes, that can scare away a man."

"What did you do for a living, Kate?"

Kate almost laughed. He had never asked her before. He would probably be surprised, since she was his "housekeeper."

"I'm an engineer, John—a safety engineer. I know that has to be a little hard to swallow, after I managed to screw up both of our lives, wrecking a car!"

John was taken back. He had not thought about her life before they met—only his. Both of their lives had changed so dramatically.

"You're kidding," he laughed. "You? An engineer? Don't you have to take a lot of firefighter's training to be a safety engineer?"

"And what's wrong with that, John Cabe?" she answered indignantly.

John heard the edge in her voice.

"Nothing—nothing's wrong with that. I just never figured—"

"You never asked," she answered curtly.

"I'm sorry, Kate. I guess both our lives have changed a lot."

She couldn't stay angry with him—not him. She knew he was a pilot and he might never fly again. He was also a computer engineer. He had lost so much.

"It's okay," she answered. "It's a surprise to a lot of people. Anyway, I did like the flowers and I like the cottage—and antiques—and children—and music!"

He laughed at her.

"I guess we do have a lot to learn about each other, don't we?"

She smiled. He seemed more comfortable than before. His lean, lanky legs were sprawled across both bar stools and rested on the legs of one. He was wearing a plaid flannel shirt and jeans. He was a very good-looking man, she thought.

Kate was still curious about the cottage, so she asked John.

"Who owned it before you, John—the cottage?"

"A couple owned it. I forget their name. They turned it over to a property management group. That's who I bought it from. The name would be on the abstract, I guess."

She was a little disappointed. He really didn't know, unless it showed up on the title work.

"John? You're going to think I'm crazy, but I just feel like I've seen that cottage before, or that I've been here before."

"Really, Kate? How could that be?"

"I don't know. It's just familiar. Anyway, it's fine. I really like it."

He was glad she had settled in so fast. He hadn't spent much time in the cottage, but he knew what she meant. It seemed that someone had taken care of it. It was the one place that he didn't have to fix anything. The plumbing worked, the paint was fresh and the furniture that was left was in excellent condition. He was curious now that Kate brought it up. He wondered about the couple that used to live there.

Dinner was ready and Kate asked John to help her set the table. At least, she wasn't going to pamper him. He had to learn his way around. The best thing Kate could think of to do was make him as independent as possible around the house.

She handed him the napkins and the silver. He carefully placed them around the table, feeling in front of each chair. Kate poured the water, and put the glasses on the table. She wondered if it would be easier to put the food directly onto the plates, so she arranged a baked potato, a pork chop, and the salad on each plate, and sat it on the table.

She called Mac inside, as she poured the coffee.

"Do either of you take cream or sugar in your coffee?" she asked them.

"No, black!" they both answered at once.

Kate laughed. She liked it the same way—black and strong.

"Then, I guess we're ready. John, tell me if you want to know where anything is. I've gone ahead and put the food on the plates. The potato is to your right, and then going clockwise, the pork chop, and the salad. The salt and pepper is in the middle of the table and the butter is to your right. I have the salad dressing here—in my hand. It's 'Ranch Dressing', if that's okay?"

Mac and John were both surprised at how efficient she was.

"Tomorrow, I'm going to find a Lazy Susan to put all of this on, and then we can just turn it around, without having to pass everything," Kate said.

"That's a good idea, Kate," laughed Mac. "Everything looks delicious. John, she's outdone herself for a first night."

John felt to see where the glass and the coffee cup were sitting. He picked up his fork and took a bite of the salad. Kate passed him the salad dressing.

"I loosened the lid, so be careful. Do you want me to—?"

He stopped her before she asked to help.

"It's fine. Don't worry. I have to learn. Thank you, Kate."

She wasn't sure if he appreciated her help, or just thought that she pitied him. She would never do that—not on purpose. He was such an independent man. Kate admired his courage and his determination.

Mac watched them. John was fine at the hospital, and Kate was more than helpful. It would just take time. Mac had noticed Kate was "walking on eggshells" around him, but he saw that in the long run, she'd be good for John. Kate made John do most of his own chores— the ones that he could do.

He knew, too, that it was hard for her—not to do things for him. Both Mac and Kate had spoken, and they were determined not to baby John Cabe.

After dinner, Kate served the pie and coffee in the living room. She placed everything on the large coffee table and picked out some old dance band CD's. Mac excused himself after eating a hearty serving of the pie.

"Thanks, Kate. John, I'm going to bed. If you need me later, just call."

They were alone. It wasn't as if they hadn't been alone before, but this time, it was different...

John told Kate how good everything tasted and then, he surprised even himself. He asked her if she would dance with him.

"I used to be pretty good, Kate," he laughed, "and if I remember this room, there's a lot of space."

She looked at the hardwood floors, and the large vacant space in front of the fireplace.

"Okay, I'm game."

She took his hand, leading him around the coffee table and into the center of the large room.

"Now, I get to lead you around," he laughed.

She gathered that he had been a person who could do anything if he put his mind to it. When he took her in his arms, she was surprised that she trembled. It wasn't from fear—she had just forgotten the touch of a man who was gentle. She tried to put away any bad thoughts of what had happened before, and just tried to relax. He made it easy.

"You are good, John," she whispered, as they danced a waltz.

The music changed. It became slower than before. Kate realized that he had pulled her closer. They danced together perfectly. She could feel every move. She inhaled, and took in his scent, and then closed her eyes. Her head rested on his shoulder. She heard his breathing deepen, and she could almost hear his heartbeat. Then, suddenly, he stopped.

"Thank you, Kate. I guess we really need to go over that schedule, don't we? I bet our coffee's cold."

Kate could have cared less about the schedule. She could have stayed right there, in his arms. What happened? Why had he stopped so abruptly?

"Oh—all right, John." She tried to sound casual. "Thanks for the dance. You really are a good dancer."

They went back over and sat on the sofa. Kate reached for some note paper and a pencil.

"Now, let's get started," she said.

She sat closer to him than before and John Cabe could smell her cologne. It smelled familiar—like jasmine and roses. He liked dancing with her—holding her. He was in control when he was doing that. He wondered what it *was* that he was feeling? When her arm touched his, as she reached for her coffee, he didn't pull back. He tried to keep talking about business. It wasn't easy. He kept visualizing the woman he rescued.

"Maureen called," he told her. "She didn't get to make it out, today."

Kate looked at him. She knew he was trying to avoid anything personal. Well, so would she!

"She said that she'd try and be here around 2:00 p.m. tomorrow, so I guess we can put that down on the schedule. She's supposed to be here Monday, Wednesday, and Friday. If we have lunch at noon, that should give us time to get ready for her visit," said Kate.

She was determined to get down to business—if that was all he wanted.

"Maureen," John whispered.

Since he had been home, John had forgotten all about Maureen. Right now, all he needed was Kate, and it scared him.

"Do you want me to fix breakfast around 8 a.m.? Or, is that too late?"

"You don't have to fix breakfast, unless you want to. I usually just have cereal anyway. Mac likes bagels or doughnuts. You could set out something the night before. That way, you could sleep in."

It suddenly became important for him to think about *her* needs. He couldn't explain what was happening here. This feeling—it couldn't be—no, not Kate...

"Oh, no. I want to fix it, she said. Breakfast early, lunch at noon, and dinner about the same time as we had it tonight. That way, both you and Matthew will have a schedule to follow. It will make it easier on him, don't you think?"

She had a point. The child needed a time for things to happen. So did he. It gave them something to look forward to and to plan around. John never thought about it much before. It seemed now that they were going to have to include everything—doctor's visits, therapies, counseling. At least, they'd stay busy! He *needed* to stay busy around Kate.

"Well, I'd better clean the kitchen. Then, I'll be out of your way. Is there anything else that you need tonight?"

John shook his head.

"Then, we can finish this schedule tomorrow, after breakfast."

John nodded. She was trying so hard. He sipped his coffee and listened to her hum to the music of the CD player, as she cleared the kitchen. He found himself wishing that she would stay there with him—all evening.

Chapter Twelve

It was almost 11:00 a.m. before John, Kate, and Mac got to check Matthew out of the hospital. The child was excited to be going home with Kate and John, even if it was just for a one-week visit. The Children's Services Social Worker had been out to check John's ranch the week before. She went over the details with Mac and made certain that both Mac and Kate would be there when the child visited.

"I'm sorry, Mr. Timmons, but I have to be certain that the child will be safe. Mr. Cabe can't possibly take care of Matthew yet. It's unfortunate. I know how much he loves the child, but the only reason I'm considering this is because Matthew is so bonded with him and with Kate Walcott. Kate and *you* will be the main caretakers, not Mr. Cabe."

Mac never told John about that conversation.

Kate and John checked out Matthew, and the boy held onto John's hand, while John held onto Kate's arm. They got Matthew into the back seat and Mac drove them back to the ranch.

"Here it is, Matthew," Mac said, as they drove up the driveway.

"Wow, it's huge," the child replied.

John and Kate grinned. The ranch was good size, but not anywhere close to "huge." It was good to be around Matthew again, and they wanted to make sure that the child had a good time while he was visiting.

"Matthew, you go with Kate. She can show you around. Mac and I will be right in. Then, we'll plan what we're going to have for lunch."

Kate smiled. Maybe John did trust her a little. She took Matthew's hand and led him up the steps and onto the porch.

"That's Old Yeller!" the child cried. "Hi, cat. I'd know you anywhere."

Matthew had already run over to the cat, and he kneeled down by the rocker.

"I love him," said Matthew. "John," he called out, "I found Old Yeller."

The cat jumped down in front of the child. He wasn't sure about this small, loud human who had invaded his space. He smelled the chubby hand, and then Matthew scratched him—right behind his ears. It must have felt good, because the cat was up in Matthew's face, requesting more scratching.

"See? He likes me. Sabrina told me he'd like me. See, Kate?"

Kate Walcott couldn't believe how this cat had affected so many lives. He had worked his way into their hearts with nothing but a snuggle—and a desire to be scratched.

If only it were so easy.

She glanced back at John, who was chatting with Mac.

It would take more than that for me to win his heart. Her thoughts surprised even Kate, as she realized that her own heart was reaching out to John Cabe.

"Come on, Matthew. Let's go inside. Yeller will follow you. Your job is going to be to feed him, while you're here with us. You can see that he gets fresh water every day. How's that?"

John Cabe heard the tail end of their conversation. It was good that Kate planned some chores for the boy. She seemed to have a knack with children, or at least with Matthew. He heard the softness of her voice, and a sudden urge to be closer to her invaded his thoughts.

After lunch, Kate and John decided to show Matthew the stables, and all the horses. Kate told Matthew that they would take the jeep. It was easier to drive John there than ask him to walk, even though the stables were close to the house. She wanted to be certain John was comfortable, especially this week.

"John's got a new colt, Matthew, and there are some horses that he wants to show you."

"That sounds like fun. Can we ride, Kate?"

"Maybe we can — tomorrow. Maybe you and I could take a couple of horses around the ranch — John, what do you think? Would it be all right?"

She didn't want to do anything without his permission. She waited for his response. She knew that he'd take the child riding himself, if he could only see.

"I think we can find a couple of mares that are gentle enough for the two of you," John replied. He smiled as he heard the boy's reply.

"Great!" the child shouted.

"Let's go and see those horses," suggested John Cabe.

Kate drove the jeep to the stables. She saw John's foreman and asked if they could tour the stables with Matthew.

Kent Able looked up and saw John climbing out of the jeep.

"Should be okay. Hello, John. It's good to see you back."

John and Kent Able spoke a few minutes while John thanked him for taking care of things while he was away.

"You may all want to be careful of that horse in the first stall. I call him 'Duke'. He's not completely broken yet. If I didn't know animals, I'd say someone had abused him. He's pretty mean...anyway, just keep your distance, okay?"

John nodded and reached for Kate. She was there, at his side, instantly. He took her arm and she grabbed Matthew's hand.

"Come on Matthew."

As they entered the Stable, Kate saw the horse Kent spoke about. He was a mustang, still partially wild, and he looked frightened as they entered.

"Stay on this side, Matthew. John, that horse looks absolutely terrified."

She guided them across from where the horse was. He snorted and jumped back and was trying to kick the back of the stall.

"It's all right boy."

Kate heard Matthew's small voice, as he took a step toward the stall.

"No! Matthew!"

Kate jerked the boy back to her side. John heard the fear in her voice.

"What is it? Is he okay?"

Kate realized she might have overreacted, but Matthew's safety was primary. Children's Services could take him back for even a small issue.

"I'm sorry, John. He's fine. Matthew, you heard what Mr. Able said. We can't get close to that horse. He's still wild. He could hurt you."

"I know. He's just scared, Kate," the boy replied. "You see that, don't you?"

Kate looked over at the horse. He *was* afraid. She didn't know why, but when she saw his eyes, she remembered what she looked like, after the rape. She recognized that look of fear.

"He is afraid," she told John, squeezing his hand.

"That doesn't keep him from being dangerous, Kate. Matthew, you mind Kate and stay back away from that stall."

"I'm sorry," the child replied.

"Come on, folks. There are some tamer horses down this way — and, you can see that new colt."

As they walked down through the stable, Kate thought of what John had just said. *"That doesn't keep him from being dangerous."* It hadn't kept her from being dangerous, either. She had wrecked her car and ruined his life in the process. Had it all been due to the fear?

"Aaaw, he's awful cute," said the boy, as they reached the stall where the new colt was.

"Yes, he is. He's reddish brown, almost the same color as your hair, Matthew — and yours, John."

She squeezed John's hand. He hadn't expected that to feel so nice. He moved closer to her, and he noticed that she didn't move away from him.

Kent Able walked toward them, from the other end of the Stable.

"Hey, folks. How do you like him?" He pointed to the new colt.

"He's a beauty," Kate answered.

She leaned over, and asked John to kneel down with her, and she put his hand on the colt's nose. It was wet and cold. John rubbed his hands up the length of the colt's head. He loved the horses. He always had. Today, he wished he could ride with Kate and with Matthew. For the first time today, he was a little sad.

"Miss Kate," continued Kent Able, "when are you going to take this young fellow for a ride?"

"We were just talking about that, Mr. Able. John suggested that you might have two gentle horses we could take out tomorrow. We wouldn't go far, just around the ranch grounds. Maybe you could show us a trail?"

"It would be my pleasure. You just let me know when you're ready. Matthew, is it?"

"Yes, sir."

"Matthew, it would be my honor to show you and Miss Kate the ranch, if Mr. Cabe doesn't mind."

John was thinking. *Mr. Cabe does mind.* He found he was a little jealous!

"Of course I don't mind, Kent," he fibbed. "You just promise to take good care of them when you go."

"Yes, sir. I'll look for you two tomorrow, then."

Kent left the stables, and Kate suggested that they leave too.

"Mac must be waiting for us."

They started back to the house. Kate watched the boy and John. They needed to be alone with each other, and get reacquainted. She pulled out some books for Matthew when they got back at the house, and asked him if he would like to read one of the stories to John and Mac. She excused herself and went to her cottage.

"I'll be back before dinner," she said to them.

As Mac and John listened to Matthew read his book, the doorbell rang.

"It's Maureen!" shouted Mac, as he answered the front door.

John had forgotten his appointment with Maureen, again.

How in the world could I have done that?

"Maureen, my favorite nurse," he said and then he heard the swish of her skirt coming toward him.

"John Cabe—my favorite patient—next to this young man. Hi, Matthew, are you enjoying your visit, so far?"

"Hi, Miss Maureen. Yes, Kate and I are going riding tomorrow and

John's cat really likes me. Kate fixed my favorite lunch—hot dogs!"

"Well," she laughed, "It sounds like you're having a grand time, Matthew. How are you, John?"

John didn't answer for a minute, and then asked Mac and Matthew if they'd excuse him for a moment. When Mac took Matthew outside, John asked Maureen to sit down. He wanted to speak to her.

"It's been better than I thought, Maureen—having Kate here. I just feel so inadequate around Matthew. It's Kate that fixes his lunch and Kate that has to take him riding. You know what I mean—things that kids like to do—I wish..."

He left the sentence unended.

"I know. It's difficult, John. Have you tried just talking to the boy? He needs someone to listen to him. He needs to talk about his parents, John. He needs *you* for that."

John had forgotten for a moment, about Matthew Clark's real needs. He was so intent on the child "having fun," he lost track of what had happened to Matthew and to his parents.

"I forgot about Matthew's loss. I've been selfish, Maureen. I've been dwelling in my own self-pity."

"Oh, no, John. It's not uncommon. You've been through a lot. But, you are just beginning to return to your life. Matthew can't –not yet. He really needs you."

"You always know what to say. Thanks, Maureen."

He didn't know how he had forgotten Maureen. He believed in her. She understood him, but then, he thought about Kate. She believed in him, too.

Maureen smiled. In her heart, she knew she was losing him, but that was what was supposed to happen. It wouldn't take much longer. That was what she was praying and hoping for. Kate Walcott was working her way into John Cabe's heart!

Kate was dusting the bedroom of the cottage when she found it— up on the top closet shelf—an old shoebox. She had to stand on tiptoe to reach it. When she pulled it down, the lid fell to the side and onto the floor. Letters and a few old papers fell out of the box.

"It wouldn't be John's," she thought. "The box is too old, and the papers and the letters inside are yellowed."

She picked up the box and sat down on her bed. She looked at one of the envelopes. It was addressed to a "Miss Katherine Turner," and the postmark was dated June 1974! She trembled as she opened the letter—Katherine Turner was her mother's *maiden* name!

John had his visit with Maureen. She checked his vitals, and told him that he was doing well. He looked so much better to her. She knew why. When she was getting ready to leave, she told Matthew that Mr. Cabe wanted to "visit" with him.

John wasn't certain how to begin. He took Matthew's hand, and led the child into his study. He started to tell Matthew about his own childhood, and showed him a scrapbook that he had stashed away on the library shelf. Matthew helped John get it down from the shelf, and they sat down on the sofa together.

The boy went through the pictures, asking John about each of them. As the child described what he saw, John would pick his memory to visualize what Matthew was seeing.

Matthew stopped when he found a picture of John and his parents.

"This must be your Mom and Dad. They kind of look like you. You're at some kind of amusement park. I see a Ferris wheel in the background."

"Oh yeah," smiled John, "I was about your age. We went to the State Fair and they asked some guy if he'd take a picture of all of us together. I remember that."

Matthew was suddenly quiet.

"Matthew? Are you all right?"

John heard the boy's voice shake when he answered him.

"I won't ever see them again, will I John?"

John put his arm around the boy.

"You're talking about your parents?"

"Yes. Right after the accident, I'd see them—you know—like they'd be right there beside me for just a minute. I'd really see them and think they were coming back. Now, I don't see them at all, except once in a while."

"But, you remember them, Matthew. You remember how much they loved you, right?"

"Yes, but it's not the same, John. I can't remember what they look like as much, anymore. I don't want to forget them—I can't!"

The boy was in tears. What could he say to help and for once in a very long time, John prayed for another person with such intensity that it even took him by surprise. He asked for wisdom with this child, as he pulled Matthew close to his chest and felt his tears on his shirt. He felt his own eyes moisten and a longing to be able to say something to the child that would help.

"Matthew, it's really hard, isn't it?"

That wasn't what he planned saying.

"Yes—it's hard."

The child was still sobbing. John reached for a tissue. Kate had put them near the sofa somewhere. He finally found them, and handed one to Matthew.

"Matthew, your parents loved you very much. I believe they still do. I think they're watching over you. You needed them so much—right after the accident; I really believe they showed up for you. That's why you saw them so clearly. They were trying to let you know that they were still here with you—so you could talk to them anytime you wanted.

"They didn't want to leave you, Matthew. They wanted to watch you grow up, and become a fine young man."

"Then, why did they leave? Why did they have to die, John? Why?"

John didn't have the answer. Why would God take away this child's

parents? Why was he blind? Why was Kate burned? He drew Matthew closer and kissed the top of his head.

"I don't know, Matthew. I don't know. I don't believe God wanted that. Maybe the driver of the other car was going too fast. Maybe that person made a terrible decision."

He thought about Kate.

"We don't know why it happened. We just have to start from here—I'll be here, Matthew. So will Kate—and Mac. We know we're not your parents, but we love you."

It wasn't what he had wanted to say, but it seemed to come from another voice, prompting him to say it. The boy hugged him. His tears stopped, at last. John and Matthew just sat there, holding onto each other for a long, long time.

Kate finished the last letter in the shoebox. Her eyes filled with tears. *I have been here before—in this very cottage!* It was with her parents. Her mother and father were the first owners of this very ranch!

She re-read the first letter.

"Darling Katherine,
I've fallen totally in love with you. I know your parents want you to go to college. They don't like me very much and they say I'm too old for you. But, I love you, Katherine. Please run away with me. Marry me.
I love you so much,
Michael Walcott, Jr."

Michael Walcott—her father. She couldn't believe what had happened. They had married in 1975. Her mother was only eighteen years old and her father was twenty-three. He was five years older, a senior in college. Her grandparents had been furious. Kate thought about her grandparents. They were rich—proper. She always thought that her own mother was so prim, but now...Kate smiled, through her tears.

Katherine had run away with him. She left *everything—her inheritance, her home—everything—for Kate's father!* She really had loved him. Kate's eyes brimmed over with tears. Her own father—he loved Katherine Turner more than Kate ever realized.

They were so happy when Kate—"Katie" was born. That was in 1978. Her parents were a young couple in love, living in this very cottage—with their new daughter. She could imagine them here. That's why she felt the love. They had made love and conceived her, right in this bedroom.

Then, the horrible tragedy—Kate closed her eyes. She could feel everything her mother had gone through. The man had come into the stable, when her father was at work. Katherine had put Katie to bed for a nap, and heard something at the back of the house. She had unlatched the door to look outside—and forgotten to lock it back.

Later, he had come into the house.

She must have been in the living room reading.

She remembered her mother reading at their home in Massachusetts. She would sit by the fire in her recliner, pull up an afghan, and lose herself in a book. She loved to read.

He found her there, catching her by surprise, just as Kate's stepfather had surprised her. The man dragged her out to the stables, and he raped her mother.

The tears were running down Kate's face, streaking her makeup, and wetting the bandage that covered her scars.

Her father had found her mother in the stable, after finding his little girl alone in her crib. He had panicked and searched the house, then outside—everywhere, until he heard her mother's moans in one of the stalls.

"My God!" said Kate, under her breath. "It happened to her, too."

Her father took her mother inside, and cared for her. According to one letter, it was months before she would let him come and sleep with her, but her father never gave up. He just kept on loving her.

Kate moaned with the grief that overcame her once again. She lay down on her bed—their bed—and grieved for her mother—for her father—for her own innocence that was taken away by some monster! She believed that she could never tell her mother what had happened to her—that her mother would never believe her. How could she have been so wrong?

"Oh, Mama—please forgive me—please forgive me for not trusting you—forgive me for thinking that you wouldn't care!"

Kate cried herself to sleep in the cottage.

Chapter Thirteen

John and Mac were playing a game of Monopoly with Matthew. John told them both that they were "cheating," since they had to read the cards to him, and count his money. He was good-naturedly accepting defeat, and the three of them were laughing. They were having a good time together, when Matthew interrupted the game.

"I'm hungry," said Matthew, hearing his tummy make a gurgling noise.

"Yes, so am I," replied John. "What time is it, Mac?"

"It's past 6:30 p.m. I wonder what happened to Kate?"

John didn't just wonder. He was worried. Kate wouldn't be late — not tonight. He asked Mac to lead him over to the cottage.

"I want to talk to her, Mac. If you'll just take me to her door, I'd like to see her alone. In the meantime, why don't you and Matthew go ahead and order us a pizza. Okay?"

"Pizza — yea!" hollered Matthew.

"Mac, could you fix us a salad, or something 'healthy', too?"

Mac grinned and said he would. He took John out the back door and led him to Kate's cottage.

"What are you thinking, John?"

"I have a bad feeling, Mac. I just know she needs me. It's like when she was in the hospital. Something's wrong. Don't ask me how I know. I just do."

Mac looked over at John's face. He was so serious. Mac knew a lot of strange things had happened since he and Nick Stewart had flown into Clarksville. He was beginning to wonder if he was in the middle of something unexplainable and he prayed for John and Kate, and somehow he knew God was watching over them.

Mac left John at the door to the cottage. John knocked, and then knocked louder. There was no answer.

"Kate? Kate!"

When he tried the door, he found it unlocked. John Cabe opened the door. He couldn't remember where all the furniture in the cottage was placed, and almost fell over a magazine rack.

"Blast! Kate? Are you in here? Kate, it's John—please answer me."

He was yelling now.

Kate Walcott sat up on the bed. She heard John calling out for her, and looked at her clock.

"Oh, no."

She got up, and ran into the living room, stumbling right into him, knocking him down, over an ottoman, and landing directly on top of him.

"Whoa, there! Kate? Are you all right?"

She struggled, as she tried to get up, and she tried to help him up.

"Oh, John…I'm so sorry. Here, let me help you."

"Never mind that. *Are you all right?*"

He was holding her by her shoulders, and she saw how worried he was. She quit trying to help him up, and instead, sat down on the floor next to him.

"I'll be fine," she said.

She didn't know how she was ever going to tell him what she found, but she knew that this was the one person she trusted more than anyone. She had to tell him.

"John? This may take awhile. I'm sorry about dinner. I cried myself to sleep, and I just woke up when I heard you call out."

"Cried? You were crying? What's wrong? I knew something was wrong. I should have come sooner."

It would have been so easy to reach over, and hold her, but he didn't. Instead, he reached for her hand, and she helped him up.

"Come in here, John. I have something difficult to tell you."

Kate led him into her bedroom, and to a chair that sat by her bed.

"Sit here. I'll try and explain what happened."

It was almost an hour later when Kate finished reading the letters, and explaining to John what had happened. He listened to her—amazed at what he was hearing.

"Kate, I can't believe this."

No wonder she cried herself to sleep. She was drained. Who wouldn't be after all she's been through? And this news? How can this be?

John got up from the chair, reached the bed and sat down beside her.

"Kate, you have to call her—you know."

"I know."

She reached for his hand, and leaned her weight against him. Then, in some miraculous way, his anger turned to forgiveness—and his forgiveness to caring—more than caring.

He had thought about her the entire time they were in the hospital. It had only increased since they came home—together. He didn't want to admit that she meant *anything* to him, but now he was finding out that she meant *everything.*

The enormity of his feelings took over, and he wrapped her in his arms, leaned down, and kissed her. Could he be falling in love with Kate Walcott?

She didn't pull away, nor did she try to resist. He was gentle—tender with her—and, despite his blindness, she felt his strength. Kate touched his face, softly at first, and then brought him closer to her. She wanted to tell him how she felt, but she held back. He would *have* to say it to her. If that happened, she would know. He felt the same as she did.

As if John heard her very thoughts, he drew back and whispered to her.

"Kate, I think I'm falling in love with you."

She held onto him tightly. Had he really said it, or had she just imagined it?

"John, please say that again. Please—say it again."

"I love you, Kate. I do. I love you."

He was trembling, and so was she. He knew he had no right to say this to her now. She was so vulnerable, and so was he, but he couldn't withhold how he felt about her any longer. This place—this cottage—and Kate—only Kate.

He traced her face with his hands. She had removed the bandages that had covered her scars, and as he felt her face, she didn't turn away, or try to withdraw.

"You're so beautiful, Kate," he said.

Kate Walcott cried. They were tears of relief and joy. John thought she was beautiful, despite the burns—despite her scars.

When Kate and John entered the ranch house, Mac knew something had happened. Kate "glowed," and John was smiling—really smiling!

"You two okay?" he asked, already knowing the answer.

He had seen that look before, on Nick Stewart's face, when he fell in love with Alexandra.

"We're fine. Where's that pizza?"

Matthew grabbed the pizza box and sat it on the kitchen table.

"It's here. When are we eating? I'm starved. Mac made a salad, John, and I helped him."

"I'm so sorry, Mac." Kate started to apologize.

"Hey, don't worry. Matthew and I did fine. We had fun, didn't we boy?"

"We did, Uncle Mac. We did."

They sat down at the table. Mac was seated at the head, Matthew on one side and Kate on the other, sitting next to John. Mac saw her take John's hand as they said grace, and he watched, as John kissed it. It was love, all right!

That evening, Matthew helped Kate with the dishes. He reminded her about their ride tomorrow. She leaned down, and planted a kiss on one of his chubby cheeks.

"I'll remember—and I promise not to oversleep. We'll go in the morning."

"It's time for bed, pardner. Come on, I'll tuck you in."

John took the child's hand, and led Matthew into the bedroom.

Kate looked at Mac and smiled. He got up, and came over to where she was standing.

"You take good care of both of them, Kate. John's just like my son. I know that he cares a lot for you. I think you kind of like him a little bit too. Am I right?"

He hugged her and she hugged him back.

"I think I love him, Mac. It's so scary."

"I know—I know. Kate, things are going to work out. I have this feeling that John Cabe is going to see again, somehow. I just know it— and you'll be there when that happens."

Kate automatically reached for the side of her face that had been burned. Mac took her hand, and placed it in his.

"You're beautiful, Kate. Don't worry. John will think so, too."

She relaxed when Mac said it. The burns had been healing well. It had even surprised her. She had one more surgery, and then Dr. Martin told her that she would look almost like her old self. She could endure it, now—as long as she had John to love her.

Maureen was at the hospital, and she felt it! She walked into Dr. Martin's office. He looked up at her and smiled.

"It's happened, hasn't it?" she asked.

"It seems to have begun," he smiled.

"Is my job finished, then?" she asked.

"No, Maureen. Kate and John will need you again—once more."

Maureen's face, which was filled with such hope, now appeared worried.

"They'll be all right, won't they?"

Dr. Martin didn't answer her. He looked toward heaven. He was saying his own prayer. It was intercession for John Cabe, Kate Walcott, and for Matthew Clark—and for this new trial they would face.

Chapter Fourteen

Kate and Matthew had a wonderful ride planned the next day. Kate was surprised that she still remembered how to sit on a horse. It had been so long since she and her father had gone riding, and Matthew was so excited. He loved the ride, too.

"Hey, Kate, watch me. I'm not bouncing so much."

She laughed at him and turned to look at Kent Able. He had two kids of his own she found out. He liked Matthew, and he taught him how to hold the reins, when to let up, and how to turn his horse. He gave the two of them the gentlest mares she had ever ridden. Kate had only one regret. She wished that John were with them.

She could envision him riding, when he was well. He would have been wonderful on a horse, and she had a sudden feeling of guilt. She had taken that away from him. How could he love her? But, he did. She felt lighter than she had in months. Tonight, she would phone her mother. Kate wished that she could see her in person. It would be easier to talk to her in person.

As Matthew and Kate were finishing the ride, they rode up to the front of the stable. As she got off the horse, she saw John. He was waiting for them, and he had a big smile on his face. She ran over to him, and put her arms around his neck.

"Hi, beautiful," he said.

It had become *her* nickname now. His best friend didn't really need it anymore. and he knew that Alexandra would understand. It slipped so easily from his mouth, he didn't question it, as he leaned down and gave her a kiss.

"The ride was wonderful. I missed you, though," she said, as she put her fingers up to brush his hair back.

He caught her wrist and kissed it.

"Did Matthew have a good time?" he asked.

"He did. He's a natural. Kent was really good with him, and Matthew was such a good listener."

"I'll have to see about him picking out his own pony," said John.

"Oh, John—his own horse? Do you think that's a good idea?"

Kate didn't want to spoil this, but she wondered if John was moving too fast. They didn't have Matthew's guardianship yet. They hadn't even been to court.

He kissed her cheek and said, "I meant he could pick out a pony to ride—whenever he visits us. Maybe later, if we get real lucky, he can pick out a horse."

"Oh, that sounds good. You're so generous, darling. That's one thing I love about you," she added, "but there's so much more."

Kate pulled his face to hers, and gave him another kiss. It was so natural. She was home at last—really home.

"You're going to make an honest man out of me yet, Kate."

John Cabe grinned down at her. He never thought he would say that to a woman.

They were interrupted by a small voice.

"Kate, John—when do we eat?"

Matthew had been standing by, watching some of this. He smiled at them and thought about what good parents they would make.

Kate laughed at Matthew.

"The boy's a bottomless pit!" she said.

"Come on. We'll go back to the house and have an early lunch."

The three of them walked the short distance to the house. She didn't mind the slower pace now, with John's hand in hers. When he put his arm around her, she felt safe.

"Well, you have a good ride?" asked Mac, as the three of them got to the front porch.

Mac was sitting on the porch swing. Yeller was in the rocker. Matthew ran up the steps and picked up the cat, then sat back down, putting him on his lap. Yeller curled back up in the child's lap.

"That cat of yours and Matthew have become inseparable," Kate said.

"I knew they'd like each other."

"You were so right. I don't know if 'like' is even the right word."

Kate and John walked up the steps and sat next to Mac.

"I'm going to start lunch. Matthew? You need to go and wash your hands. I need your help fixing lunch, okay?"

"Okay. Yeller, I'll go get your food and water first. I have to help Kate."

The child and the cat followed her into the house.

"That's something," smiled Mac. "She's a lot like the 'pied piper'. They just follow her anywhere."

John laughed, "So would I. She could ask me to go anywhere, and I'd do it. I guess you've figured out I'm pretty much 'taken' with her."

"It doesn't take much to figure that out, John. I wish you could see your face. You've got a grin a mile across. You're falling in love with her, aren't you?"

"I think I am, Mac. I think I am."

"Wow! That's heavy, John. This has happened awfully fast, hasn't it?"

"I know that, Mac. I also know that the circumstances that should have divided us, drew us together instead. That's kind of miraculous in itself."

"Funny you said that. I've been thinking a lot about miracles these days. It started some time back, when Alexandra was so ill—remember? I remember the change that Nicholas went through. I'm seeing that in you, John—almost the same thing."

John felt a chill run through him. He remembered all too well when Alex almost died, when he prayed for her and when Nick Stewart went through some kind of an amazing transformation. Of course, she had lived, but John always knew it was a miracle. First, his two best friends—now, Alexandra's new baby—he just hadn't thought about it—Kate and Matthew—were they to be his own miracles?

He wondered about God. If God didn't want this to happen, who else?

"I haven't been one to talk much about my faith, Mac. I prayed mostly in a crisis. That's about the only times. Today, I find myself thanking Him for all kinds of things. Can you believe that? I'm blind—but I'm seeing more of God than I ever have. Maybe, I was too busy before to really see Him."

It had been a wonderful day so far, and when Kate picked up the phone, she wondered how she would begin. She was in John's study, and she dialed her mother's phone number.

"Mom?" she began.

"Kate? Katie?"

The voice on the other end of the line was almost a whisper. Kate knew that her mother had been crying. She had not talked to her since the crash. Her mother got her reports only through Dr. Martin after that. She didn't know if the police had contacted her about the report, or not.

Kate's eyes filled with tears, at the sound of her mother's voice.

"Katie, are you all right? Where are you?"

Kate Walcott couldn't imagine her mother's reaction when she explained that she was living at John Cabe's ranch—and in his cottage out back.

"You're *where?*"

Kate heard her mother's gasp.

"Mom, I have something else to tell you."

It all came tumbling out—the trip she made to reason with her stepfather—what he had done to her—her attempted suicide—John's blindness—her burns.

Her mother was sobbing on the other end of the line. Kate could talk no more. The two people on the phone tried to *feel* what the other was thinking.

Finally, Kate's mother spoke.

"Oh, Katie—what have I done? What have you been through? You must hate me!"

"Mom, the only person I hate is myself—for not talking to you. But, Mom, there's more—I've saved the best for last. Out of all of this nightmare, there has been so much good that has come from it."

She told her mother about finding the letters. She wasn't sure how her mom would react.

"Katie? You found them there—where you are right now?"

"Yes, Mom. Right here."

"I thought they were lost forever. I remember going over the cottage with a fine toothcomb when I returned for a visit. I never found them. You must have been destined to find them, Katie. I'm so glad that you did. They brought *you back to me.*"

Kate smiled, "Mom, they also brought me to John."

"What do you mean?" her mother asked, incredulous of all that had happened to her daughter.

"I mean he loves me, Mom—he really loves me—burns and all— and, I love him Mama—more than you'll ever know. He's such a good man, Mom. I can't wait for you to meet him."

"Katie, are you sure? Are you certain it isn't the guilt you feel—the pity for this man?

"No!" Kate almost shouted.

She was determined that her mother knew she had never felt pity for John. All the time she was sorrowful for what had happened, he had remained her strength.

"Mom, you have to know him. He's a strong, fine person. Believe me, it isn't pity that sends this electricity through me when he touches me. It's not pity when I feel his touch. I love him so much, Mama."

Katherine Turner Walcott paused. She heard an echo in her daughter's voice that resonated her own—years ago—when she had explained how she felt to her own parents. She softened immediately.

"Katie, I'm so happy for you, darling. I can't wait to meet your John Cabe."

Kate heard the acceptance in her mother's voice. It had come, full circle.

John knew that Kate was speaking to her mother. He prayed for her the entire time that she was in his study. He knew how rough it would be—to tell her mother about the rape—the suicide attempt— and then, the letters. He wondered if Kate would tell Katherine about him? The woman would have a lot to digest. He prayed she would be kind to his Kate. How could she be any other way?

John heard the door close, as Kate came from the study. Her face would have told the story, if John could have seen her. Instead, she walked to him and laid her face against his chest, holding onto him.

"Kate?" He pulled her closer. "Are you all right?"

"More than all right. I think I must be dreaming, John. My mother was wonderful. It was as if she heard me for the first time."

John said a silent "Thank You" to the God he was just beginning to know. He leaned down and took her face in his hands, and kissed her—gently at first, and then with a passion he had, long before he ever admitted he loved her.

When he released her, both of them took a deep breath.

"Wow!" Kate said.

"Yes, I felt that too," he told her.

"Perhaps we better sit down. I don't expect to be knocked off my feet that often," Kate smiled and she knew for certain that he truly loved her.

They sat on the sofa, in front of the fireplace, and talked. They listened to Mac and Matthew banter about lunch. They told each other everything about the other. John laughed, as Kate spoke of her tomboy experiences as a child—getting caught in a tree and swinging down, breaking an arm. She grinned, as John told her about learning to ride his first bike, and how many bruises he had. His parents had counted thirty-nine black and blue marks on his legs, but he wouldn't give up.

"I don't give up easily, Kate, when I want something."

She trembled when he said it. He wouldn't give up on her, either. He wouldn't give up trying to conquer his blindness, and he wouldn't give up trying to get Matthew.

She rested back against his arm, and they sat silently for a long time. There was no need for words.

It was close to the weekend. Matthew had to be returned to the hospital, and all of them were dreading his leaving. Kate fixed Matthew's favorite breakfast—pancakes and sausages—but no one ate much.

"It will work out, son," John told the boy.

"I don't want to leave," Matthew whined. "I like it here—with you and Kate and Mac." He picked up the cat, "I'll miss you, Yeller."

139

It was all they could do to keep from breaking down right in front of the child, but the adults managed a brave front, and finally, they were in the jeep, headed back to the hospital.

"I'll see if you can visit us in a few days, Matthew," John promised him.

"Of course, we'll visit you in the Children's Wing, until then," added Kate.

"Of course we will—I plan winning back all of that Monopoly money, Matthew," said John.

"I'm going to pray to the angel," said Matthew, "She'll help me."

"What angel, Matthew?"

Kate and John were both curious.

"Sabrina's angel. She told me she talked to her. She told Sabrina that you'd be able to see again, John. I figure that she'll help me too, if I just believe in her."

John gulped. He had a large lump in his throat. Kate was silent, but she squeezed his hand. For some reason, they both thought of Maureen McConnell.

"I hope Maureen's on duty today," said Kate.

John was thinking the same thing. She was always so good with Matthew. She had helped him—and Kate. He hadn't told Maureen about his feelings for Kate.

Will she be surprised when I tell her about Kate and me.

They arrived at the hospital and got out of the Jeep. When they walked into the Children's Unit, Dr. Martin was waiting.

"Matthew, welcome back. Did you have a good visit?"

"I did, but I hate coming back. Can't I stay with John and Kate longer?"

"If it were up to me, Matthew, I'd let you go back right now. I guess we're going to have to convince the lady from Children's Services that very same thing."

Dr. Martin smiled at Kate and John.

"You two look wonderful. Anything I should know?"

They both stood in front of him, holding hands, grinning ear to ear. There was no way in the world they could keep this secret.

"Well, you might say that we've made up," grinned John.

"Aaww!" interrupted Matthew. "They're in love. Can't you see it?"

They all broke out in laughter. Dr. Martin was smiling at all of them.

"I guess I can see that, Matthew. I was hoping for that, you two."

"It just kind of hit us," continued John Cabe, "like a bolt out of the blue—if you know what I mean."

Dr. Martin almost laughed. He knew exactly what John meant.

"I think I know, John. Maureen will be elated! She's been praying for this since you two first arrived."

"Is she here today?" asked Kate, "I'd like to see her and tell her."

"She's around here somewhere. I'll try and find her. I think she's supposed to be out to your place this afternoon, anyway."

"Oh, yes," said John, realizing he had forgotten again.

Dr. Martin grinned. He knew the more Kate grew in John Cabe's life, the less John would need Maureen. Still, Maureen had at least one more important assignment. It was one that neither Maureen, nor Dr. Martin, was looking forward to.

John received the news in the mail the following week. Children's Services had denied him guardianship "at the present time." They had questions about the child's safety due to "Mr. Cabe's limitations and physical handicap."

When Mac read the letter to John, he saw the look on his face. It was not only one of disappointment. It was filled with anger.

"I'm sorry, John, but it doesn't say that Matthew can't visit. In fact, they don't have anyone right now who will take him with his psychological problems right now. Mrs. Nichols told us he could come back out here next week. I'm sure we can work out something."

Mac became even more worried when he didn't answer him. John got up, walked to his bedroom, and closed his door. It was then, that Mac phoned Kate.

"Kate? Can you come right over? I need to talk to you."

Chapter Fifteen

Kate couldn't imagine what Mac wanted. It was right after breakfast, and she had just returned to the cottage from the main house. She was trying to get the cottage cleaned for her mother's visit, and she wanted it to look exactly the same as when her mother lived here. Katherine's visit was only three days away. John was going to send his jet to pick up her mom. The new pilot that Mac had hired was working out well, and Kate's mother was excited to be coming to see her—and to meet John Cabe.

Kate locked her door, ran up the steps of the main house, and walked through the back door. She wore jeans and a light blue t-shirt, and her auburn hair shone with gold highlights from the sun, while her green eyes sparkled with excitement. It had been a good week for her.

"Mac? Where are you?" she called out, as she entered.

Mac came out of the study, motioning her to be quiet. When she saw his face, she knew something was wrong.

"What is it? Is something wrong with John?"

"Kate. We've had some bad news."

He handed her the letter that John had dropped on his way out of the living room.

As Kate Walcott read, her countenance changed from the lightness she had been feeling to one of anger and disappointment.

"They can't do this!" she exclaimed. "They can't do this to Matthew or to John."

"I tried to tell John that at least the boy's visits haven't stopped. You know he expected more, Kate. He loves that little boy. He was thinking about adopting him. He's crushed—as you can imagine."

Kate thought about John...he didn't need this, not now. Things were just beginning to look up for him. She crumpled the paper in her hand and threw it on the floor.

"Well, we'll just see about this, Mac. We will just see. Who's the Judge on this case? I want to talk to someone—and it won't be a social worker!"

Mac had seen Kate depressed. He had seen her happy, but he had never seen Kate Walcott this angry. She was formidable. Mac stepped back a bit while she ranted. He thought about Sabrina Stewart. Kate and Sabrina had the same determination. They were two people who didn't take "no" for an answer, if they thought they were right.

Mac watched her—the fire in those green eyes. *I'd hate to oppose her. Well, maybe this situation needs a 'little fire'!*

Kate walked to the phone and called the County Court House. When she hung up, she had an appointment with Judge Tolbert Nichols, Matthew's judge.

"Where's John?" she asked.

Mac pointed to the bedroom, and watched her as she stormed in. She didn't even knock. Mac just had to smile. This was a Kate Walcott that he didn't know, but he thought he liked her!

Kate found John sitting on the edge of his bed across from the back yard window. Although he couldn't see the sunlight streaming in the window, he could feel its warmth. His shoulders were slumped, and he had put his head in his hands.

"John?"

He started to ask Kate to leave, but he couldn't do that. He needed her now, more than ever. She walked over to him and sat down, putting her arms around him. As he leaned against her, she took a deep breath.

"We haven't lost him, John. I won't let that happen. Believe me! You have to believe me. I won't let it happen. I promise you that."

John turned toward her. He heard an earnest plea in her voice that he had heard before—from Maureen and from Alex—saying the same thing. *"Believe me. I'll always tell you the truth...believe me...believe."*

He had believed. They had never lied to him. Now, Kate was asking the same thing.

"I believe you, Kate," he heard himself saying to her.

She held his face in her hands and kissed him.

"I have an appointment with Judge Nichols in the morning. Will you come with me?" she asked.

It surprised him. Why had he caved in so fast? Kate was taking action, at least. It was what he needed to do.

"I'll go, of course, I'll go," he told her.

"Good. I have an idea. I need to talk to you about it first."

When they came out of the bedroom, Mac knew something had happened. John looked better and Kate looked determined. They both sat down at the kitchen table and grabbed a pencil and paper.

"Mac? We're going to need coffee—lots of coffee," Kate said.

"Sure. You know I make it pretty strong."

"Good!" Both of them replied at the same time.

"The stronger, the better, Mac," John said.

Mac didn't know exactly what was going on, but he knew they were planning something.

"Kate? Are you certain that you want to do this?" John asked.

"I've never been so certain, John."

"But we really don't know how this is going to work out. We barely know each other. We may be rushing into something we wished we hadn't."

She looked disappointed when he said it. At least, he couldn't see her. Maybe this was a crazy idea. Maybe, he was right. They hadn't known each other but a few weeks. John had never even seen her after the wreck. She thought about her burns and all the old doubts came flooding back, but then, she remembered Matthew and she knew they had to do this for him—if for no other reason.

"I'm sure John. We have to do this for Matthew."

"For Matthew," he agreed.

Judge Tolbert Nichols didn't usually make appointments with citizens involved in any of his cases, but this was Michael Walcott's daughter. Judge Nichols was an old friend of Michael Walcott's. It had been so many years ago that he and Mike were beginning their careers. He wondered how Katherine was. She was such a beautiful woman back then. He hadn't seen her since she and Mike left Clarksville. So—this was her child—the little girl, Katie Walcott.

Tolbert Nichols remembered the child. She had her mother's red hair. He may have been the only one, other than her parents and the man, who knew what had happened to her mother. He owed Michael Walcott at least this much—to hear his daughter out.

He hadn't been able to do anything to help her mother. The man got off—scot-free! As a young attorney, he was unable to prevent it. Tolbert never forgave himself for losing that case. It wasn't long after that before Katherine and Michael moved away.

Now, Katie Walcott was back home. The Judge smiled.

John and Kate sat outside Judge Tolbert Nichol's office in a small waiting room. They were early for their appointment. Kate dressed in a cream-colored suit that she had bought only yesterday. After her hospitalization, it was the first time she had been inside a department store. She only ordered jeans and slacks before and she always had them delivered. Today, she wanted to look business-like and sure of herself. So much depended on this!

Kate used to dress up a lot. She knew the most powerful men in Boston. She dealt with them like she had her suicide attempt—she crushed them! Kate had been ruthless in her business dealings at one time. She couldn't believe that part of her life. Everything had changed so much. She never wanted to go back to that life—not ever!

John sat next to her, dressed in one of the few suits he had left, after leaving California and moving to his ranch in Arizona. Kate glanced over at him. He was nervous, but he looked wonderful to her. His soft brown suit matched his eyes—the eyes she hoped would see her someday.

Judge Nichols' court clerk came out and showed them inside his chambers. They were now face to face with Tolbert Nichols.

"Mr. Cabe? Miss Walcott? Please, sit down."

Tolbert Nichols was amazed at the likeness—the auburn hair, the fair skin and those green eyes—She looked exactly like her mother! Except for the fact that she was taller, it was as if he were looking at Katherine Spencer again—over twenty-five years ago. He remembered a time when they were in high school and he was in love. He cleared his throat and took a drink of water.

"May I offer you something?"

He was a pleasant looking man, Kate thought. He sort of reminded her of her own father. His gray hair was salt and pepper and he was tall. Underneath his black robes, she saw a large frame, but he wasn't too heavy. Tolbert Nichols was very handsome, indeed.

"No, thank you," both Kate and John replied.

"Judge Nichols, I'll get right to the point."

When didn't you, Katherine? He smiled, thinking of Kate's mother.

He realized he was staring at her—same build—same spirit as her mother.

"It's about Matthew Clark, the boy at Saint's Hospital. The child's parents were killed in an accident."

"Yes, I remember the case. My sister is the social worker on it. It was terrible. I've seen Matthew. I went to the hospital right after his parents died."

This surprised Kate and John. The judge's sister is "Ms. Nichols"? Most judges didn't remember their cases. They just had too many, but this one had actually visited?

"We've—John—Mr. Cabe has filed for guardianship, Your Honor. We received this letter from Children's Services—from your sister."

Kate had to hand him a crumpled piece of paper. She explained that she was the one who had mistakenly thought that it was trash and threw it away.

First lie to a Judge, Kate thought.

The Judge smiled, and read the letter. Then, he laid it down and looked at John.

"Clearly, Mr. Cabe. You have to understand their reasoning."

"But it isn't the case, Your Honor!" Kate said.

John interrupted her, squeezing her hand. She quieted, and let him speak.

"I love Matthew, Your Honor. He loves me—and he loves Kate. I explained that Kate is there. She lives in the cottage right behind my house. She's there all the time to help care for Matthew. There's also Mr. Timmons. He lives with me. It's not as if I have to care for Matthew all by myself."

"And," Kate drew in a deep breath—ready to say what they had planned, "we're getting *married*, Your Honor! So, you see—Matthew will have both a mother and a father. I love him too, Judge Nichols. We both do. This is killing us—it's killing Matthew. He fell for John the first time he met him—and vice-versa! You have to intervene, Your Honor. You just have to. To have that child love someone after he's lost both of his parents—well, that in itself is a miracle!"

Kate Walcott finally took a breath, and Judge Tolbert Nichols smiled. She had her mother's determination, all right. He shuffled some papers on his desk.

"I'll have to make a home visit," he replied, "and I'm not promising anything—I want to speak to Matthew too. When are you getting married?"

John spoke up.

"In three days, Your Honor—when Kate's mother visits us."

Tolbert Nichols felt his face flush. He wasn't easily distracted, but this news—Katherine coming back here, in three days? He had a perfect opportunity to see her again. He had to make a home visit, didn't he?

"Three days away, huh? That sounds good. Will Matthew be attending?"

"We haven't told him yet, Your Honor," said Kate.

She looked over at John. Would this spoil it? They hadn't told Matthew! God, what were they thinking?

John Cabe smiled at her, and then he spoke.

"We wanted to surprise him. He's been on us to get married, so he could live with us."

Lie number two. Kate winced.

"I'm sure he'll be pleased, then. I'll try and make arrangements to visit him tomorrow. I'd like to make a home visit before you go on your honeymoon. Would it be terrible of me to invite myself to your wedding?"

Tolbert Nichols could not believe what he had just asked of them—intrude on their wedding day, just so he could see Katherine?

"We'd love to have you, Judge Nichols," Kate answered. "In fact, we don't have a pastor yet. Would you consider doing the wedding? It certainly would help with all of the paper work too."

John couldn't believe what he was hearing.

Kate—are you out of your mind? Have you "lost it"?

"I'd be delighted, Katie—Miss Walcott. I have to confess something to you. I knew your father, Kate. We used to be good friends, a long time ago. I knew your mother in high school. I look forward to seeing her, again. I didn't mean to be dishonest with you."

Kate was astonished. How lucky could they be? Surely, he'd let them have Matthew—surely, now—and she thanked God for one more miracle!

"You look so much like your mother, Kate," Judge Nichols smiled at her and then turned to John Cabe.

"Mr. Cabe, you may think I don't know your background, but believe me, I do. I'm honored to meet you, Sir. Did you know you're marrying a hero, Kate? I bet he hasn't even told you."

John hadn't, but Mac had. Kate knew John's history with terrorists, and with Nicholas and Alexandra Stewart. She put her arm in his.

"I know how lucky I am, Judge Nichols. Believe me, I know."

John squeezed her arm. She had done it! He knew she had convinced this man—under all these circumstances. What were the chances? John Cabe said his own "Thank You" to the One who had arranged all of these events—to his newly found Lord and Savior.

Chapter Sixteen

Nicholas Stewart couldn't believe Mac's phone call. He yelled up the stairs to Sabrina and Alexandra, telling them to 'hurry up and get downstairs!'

"You're not going to believe this!" he yelled out.

Alex was in the middle of fixing Sabrina's hair for school. They could have heard Nick from anywhere in the mansion when he called to them. She wondered what had happened, put down the hairbrush, and both she and her daughter started down the stairway.

"What in the world—Nick, you're yelling at the top of your lungs—what is it?"

"What's going on, Daddy?"

Sabrina was out of breath, as her small legs tried to keep up with her mother down the stairs.

"Uncle Johnny's getting married!" he shouted.

Nick Stewart couldn't believe what he had just said, but that was what Mac told him.

"What did you say?" asked Alexandra.

Alex said a prayer that her husband wasn't having some kind of attack, or playing a joke on them.

"It's true, Alex. Mac just phoned. John and Kate Walcott are getting married. They want us there, and the wedding is in two days!"

"What?" Alex was stunned.

"In two days—and that's not all..."

He helped his wife sit down. She looked a little dizzy, and Sabrina was jumping up and down like a jack-in-the-box, so he had to settle her down, too. He picked up Sabrina, and then sat down next to his pregnant wife.

"Okay, let's all calm down."

He was addressing himself, as much as anyone. He took a deep breath and took Alexandra's hand. She looked flushed.

"Are you all right, honey?"

"I think so. It's just—tell us again Nick—slowly."

He put Sabrina down, next to him, and held onto her hand so that she wouldn't get up from the sofa.

"Mac said that Kate and John have fallen in love. The main reason that they're marrying this fast is because of Matthew."

"My Matthew?" asked Sabrina.

Sabrina now claimed her friend as her very "own" Matthew.

"Yes, Sabrina—*your Matthew*," her father replied.

"How does this involve Matthew?" Alex asked.

"John and Kate want to adopt him. Because of John's condition, they were about to tell him that he couldn't have Matthew. Kate offered, Alex. She offered to go ahead and marry John, so that they could give the child a home."

"But, how does she feel about John?"

"Mac says they're as in love with each other as you and I were—not that I believe that's possible, but Mac says they really love each other."

"See Daddy, I told Matthew if he'd pray to my angel, he'd get to go live with Uncle Johnny and Kate. Mommy, I told him that he just needed to believe—really believe."

Alexandra went over to her daughter and hugged her.

"Oh, Sabrina, I love you. You have so much faith. I wish I were more like you."

"Oh, Mommy—you have faith. You're just a grown-up, and it

takes a little longer."

Nick and Alex had to smile. She was so honest—and it was so true.

"So, we have to be there two days from now? Are you telling me they're having the wedding at the ranch?"

"Yes. From what I heard, Kate's mother is coming. Other than that, it's you and me and Mac—Matthew, of course, and you, Sabrina—and the Judge that they're having marry them—get this, Alex—this is the Judge that's making a decision on the adoption!"

"Whoa, Nicholas—that's just too weird!"

"Weird? Or, miraculous?"

"It has to be Dr. Martin and Maureen's work…"

"I don't think so. Remember what they said to us? They just bring the people together—what happens from there has to be their own choice."

"You're right, Nick. It's so—so"

She had no words for it.

"Is it a miracle, Mommy?"

"Yes, Sabrina. I think it is. It's a miracle."

Alexandra's eyes filled with tears as she thought of her unborn child. Nick came over, and put his arms around his family, as he touched Alexandra's stomach. He knew what a real miracle was.

"I'd say we have to think about getting ready. Alex, will you phone Sabrina's teacher? I'll call my pilot. You go and pick us out something to wear. Mac says dressy, but informal—I guess that means—I don't know what that means!"

Alex laughed at her husband. She hadn't seen him this excited since they found out about the baby.

"Don't worry, darling. I'll take care of it. Go and take care of the pilot."

Sabrina giggled.

"He's really happy, Momma."

"Yes, Sabrina. He really is."

Mac Timmons hung up the phone. It was good to hear from Nick again. Soon, Mac would return there—to live with his other family— his other boy. Right now, John still needed him, but soon—he wouldn't. He'd have his own family.

Mac prayed that John's eyesight would return. He knew Dr.

Martin thought it was psychological, but John had forgiven Kate—
there had to be some other reason, but what?

When John and Kate told Matthew that they were getting married
and that they wanted him to come and live with them, he rolled out
of the hospital bed and grabbed them both by the knees, hugging
them so tightly, he nearly knocked them over.

"I love you both so much," the child cried.

"Son," John said, "We still have to wait for a Judge to decide if you
can stay with us, but we're very hopeful. We love you too, Matthew."

"We do, Matthew—both of us love you so much. We want you at
our wedding. It's two days from now. The Judge will be there. He
may drop by here, too, Matthew. He wants to talk to you. His name is
Judge Nichols."

"I remember him. He came to see me—before. He was kind of nice,
Kate."

"I think he is nice, Matthew. All you have to do is tell him the truth.
He only wants the best home for you. I hope he picks ours."

"He has to, Kate. John, I want to live with you and with Kate.
Please."

"Matthew, let's ask God about it? Would that be all right? Right
now—you and I and Kate. We'll say a little prayer and ask God if he'll
let you come home with us."

John Cabe had never asked anyone to pray with him, except Nick
or Alex before. He felt a little awkward, but he knew it was right. Kate
took his hand and Matthew took the other one. They formed a small
circle, right there in the Children's Unit. Then, they prayed...

Maureen glowed, as she watched them. She had become so close
to these humans—almost too close. It would be difficult to leave. Dr.
Martin slipped in quietly, right behind her.

"It's what we've been waiting for, Maureen," he said.

"I know. It's wonderful. But, this next trial—so soon—do you
think...?"

"Maureen. Do I hear worry in that voice?"

Dr. Martin was right. She confessed her fear immediately, as a
bright light appeared before them. She knew then, they would all
break through the darkness!

"Fear NOT!"

She heard an audible voice—One she knew—One who knew her.

Dr. Martin's head lifted toward the heavens and he raised his hands toward the light.

"Thank you, Lord," he whispered, "Give us strength to continue. Help us to help them—Your will be done, Father."

"Amen," whispered Maureen.

Chapter Seventeen

Mac dropped Kate off at one of the local shops in Clarksville. She asked him to pick her up in a couple of hours.

"I have a million things to do, Mac—a million! My mother will be here tomorrow and I have to fix the house and I don't have a wedding dress. We need groceries and a cake and..."

She was tired from just agonizing over it. What had they been thinking? A wedding in three days? Now, it was down to two!

"Kate, you just concentrate on the dress," Mac replied. "I've been shopping for Nick Stewart for years. I think I can manage a few groceries and a wedding cake. You go get your dress. I'll do the rest."

"Oh, Mac, what would we ever do without you? Thanks so much. I need something for dinner tomorrow night when Mom's here, and then—well, I thought a cake and punch for the wedding, but I need some kind of party food for a buffet—for our guests."

"Got it!" Mac laughed at her excitement.

"Kate?" he continued.

"Yes?"

"Watch it—you're glowing."

She grinned, "I know I'm too tense, Mac. I'll just leave it to you and we can go over the rest when I meet up with you later. I'll see you in a couple of hours."

Mac watched her, as she disappeared into the department store. He had to smile. She was the best thing that had come into John's life in a long time.

As Kate walked through the store, she thought of all the things she had to purchase. She walked to the women's department, and looked through the dresses.

Not right…not right…wrong color.

"May I help you, Miss?"

A young girl walked over to her.

"I'm looking for a dress—a very special dress—to wear to a wedding. I'm afraid I don't see anything that looks—the way I want it to look."

"Is it an afternoon, or an evening wedding?"

"It's early afternoon. It's going to be outside, near a rose garden."

Kate thought of the side yard, where she and John would marry. He planted roses on that side—and lilacs. In the morning, it was in full sun, but by afternoon, the shade caught it and it was filled with trees. It was lovely. The wedding would be casual, but she wanted to wear something that John would like—if he could see her—something soft, and feminine.

"We have more dresses over here."

The girl led her to another department. She told Kate that she had something in the back she wanted her to see.

Kate searched through the dresses and gowns on the rack. There was one lace gown in a light blue that wasn't too bad. Then, the clerk reappeared—carrying out two gowns.

The first was aqua in color, and in a fabric that resembled gauze. It was lovely. Kate touched it. It would feel good when John touched it. That was important. Then, she picked up the other, and she knew she had found the dress she would be wearing. She took it from the girl.

"Oh, it's beautiful," she whispered.

"I like that one, too. It'll look great on you, with your auburn hair and your coloring. Go ahead—take both of them back and try them on."

Kate took both dresses back into the dressing room. She only tried on the one she had fallen in love with.

"Please, let it fit," she prayed.

The dress was silk. It was a soft ivory color, with an overlay of floral chiffon that had pale turquoise and lavender flowers. There were light green leaves that appeared to fade right into the folds, and it seemed to change colors, as she moved. Someone had sewn individual seed pearls around the neckline. The dress flowed, as Kate slipped into it. It fit her perfectly, and it was the softest fabric that she had ever touched.

"I love it," she said to the girl who had helped her. "Now, I need everything else—lingerie—shoes—jewelry—the works!"

She laughed when she saw the expression on the clerk's face.

"I'm the bride," she laughed, "and, our wedding's day after tomorrow."

Almost two hours later, Kate walked out of the store with her arms loaded with packages. Mac saw her heading toward the car and jumped out to help her.

"Looks like you bought out the place, Kate."

"I think I did—but, Mac—I found the most wonderful dress, and shoes that match—and pearls, and lingerie…"

Mac laughed. Kate was bursting with excitement.

"I got the cake ordered. I can pick it up tomorrow afternoon. The groceries are in the car. I think I got everything, Kate. You may want to check the bags."

"I'm sure you did fine, Mac. What about candles…and flowers?"

"I think you're going to find out your future husband has already taken care of that—and he hired a caterer to serve us and make sure everything is just perfect. John Cabe is quite the romantic underneath the gruff exterior."

"Oh, Mac—I never found him gruff. He's perfect. He got flowers, candles, and a caterer, huh?"

"Yes, and champagne, for the punch."

"Bless him, Mac. I don't know about you, but I'm exhausted. Let's go home! I need coffee bad!"

Mac Timmons threw his head back and laughed. Coffee was their anecdote for almost everything.

The next morning, Kate drove John to the edge of the airstrip. She watched, as his pilot landed the jet, and her mother got off the plane.

Kate asked John to wait by the car, while she went to get her mother.

"Mom! Over here!"

"Kate—Katie! Oh, I'm so glad to see you!"

Katherine Walcott hugged her only daughter and then looked her over.

"You've lost weight, child, but you look good!"

Kate was relieved. Her mother hadn't even mentioned her face.

Katherine Turner Walcott stared at her child as if she had never seen this young woman before. Her child was in love, and she had never seen her happier. Where were the scars that she had told her about? She saw only an Ivory complexion, with a slight blush to it. It was flawless! Kate was beautiful!

Kate picked up her mother's suitcase, and led her mother back to where John Cabe stood, waiting for them.

"Mom, this is John."

Kate beamed as she said it.

John extended his hand, and Katherine Walcott placed her hand in his.

"Mr. Cabe. It's so good to meet you. I can't tell you how happy I am for you, and for my Katie."

"Mrs. Walcott, I've heard a lot of good things about you from Kate. I'm glad you could be here. I know this has happened really fast. I want to get to know you. I hope that we can talk later."

Katherine Walcott saw what her daughter had seen in this man. He was a kind man—she knew that from what Kate had told her. There was something in his manner that made an instant connection with her, too. As she climbed in the back seat of the car, she saw her Katie lean over and kiss his cheek. It was the warmest feeling Katherine had sensed in a long time.

Katherine sat back in the car and watched the highway disappear, as they drove up the gravel road that led into the ranch's driveway.

How long has it been since I've been here? The last time I was here was without Michael. It was to check out the houses and see what the last set of renters had done to them.

She remembered hunting for the letters and the pictures even then. She was certain that she had checked the closet where Katie had found them. Why then, had they suddenly appeared for her, when Katherine had not ever seen them?

Old memories came flooding back when she saw the ranch house. Someone had planted roses and lilacs—even honeysuckle. The place looked nice. John and Kate removed her luggage and Kate motioned her to the house.

"Come on, Mom, I've fixed a dinner you won't believe," said her daughter.

"We'll go put your luggage up and then come back here. You have to meet Mac and *this* is Old Yeller."

Katherine looked at the cat. She had no feelings for animals, one way or another.

Poor scraggly beast...He is pretty fat, though.

"Looks like he needs to be put on a diet, Kate. What have you been feeding him?"

"Mom, *everyone's* been feeding him. That's the problem!"

Kate laughed, and poked John in the ribs. She knew how he snuck food under the table for the cat.

Mac Timmons came from the kitchen, apron on, and towel in hand.

"Mom, this is Mr. Timmons—Mac..."

"Pleased to meet you, Ma'am," he replied.

Mac tried to "read" Katherine Walcott. She was a fine looking woman, but something was missing. She didn't have the softness that he saw in Kate. Katherine wasn't cold, but he noticed that she didn't warm up to people easily. There was sadness there too. He hoped that John was on her "good side." Mac decided she could be a formidable opponent, if she wanted.

Kate led Katherine out the back door, to her cottage. She heard her mother take a deep breath, as they entered. Kate had cleaned, washed, and dusted everything there. It was spotless!

"Here, Mom," she said, "I'll let you have the bedroom, and I'll sleep on the sofa."

"Nonsense, Katie, I'm used to sleeping on our couch at home. I'll do it here, too. Besides, if you think I'm going to put you out of your bed on the night before your wedding, you're mistaken."

Katherine Walcott was used to getting her own way, so her daughter didn't try to overrule her. She watched, as her mother left the living room and explored the cottage. Kate followed closely behind her.

"I see you've turned the second bedroom into an office, dear."

"Oh, den, office, private space—whatever you want to call it. Do you like it?"

"It's fine," she answered, "if it meets your needs. I see you haven't made any other changes, Katie."

"No, Mom, it was all perfect—just the way it was."

For one moment, she thought she saw her mother smile. It must be hard, remembering all the joy—and the horror of this place.

"Your father and I had the happiest times of our lives in this place, Katie. That's what I want you to remember. You were so little."

Kate watched the tears begin in her mother's eyes. She went over to her and put her arms around her.

"It's okay, Mom. I understand."

Katherine couldn't believe that her daughter was comforting her. It should be the other way around. Kate—her Katie—she had been through so much. How could she be so calm?

"Well, this is just silly," said Katherine, wiping away her tears. "We have to get back to that nice young man of yours, and I'm looking forward to your dinner, Katie."

Katherine Walcott had managed to dismiss the rape and her daughter's pain at the same time. Kate knew she would never bring it up again.

The dinner went well. Even Katherine had to admit that her child had become a fine cook, and she liked John Cabe. It was funny. He reminded her of Michael, Katie's father. Perhaps, it was his calm demeanor. She smiled at them. He was the direct opposite of her Katie.

Katie had been so "no-nonsense" in her business dealings, staying up all hours of the night, and talking on the phones to close a deal. When she looked at her now, she would never find that Kate. She had changed—thought Katherine—and she liked her daughter better now.

"So tell me about the wedding, John. Who else is coming? Who's marrying you two?"

John told Katherine about the Stewarts and Matthew. Kate watched, as her mother's face lit up. John had managed to impress her when he mentioned Nicholas Stewart's name. Then, he told her that Judge Tolbert Nichols would be performing the ceremony. Kate saw that expression, too. Her mother's face grew flushed.

"Judge Tolbert Nichols?" her mother asked.

"Yes, Mom. He said that he knew you."

"Yes, we went to high school together. It's been a while since I last saw him."

Katherine's mind was spinning.

"Bert, why now, after all these years?"

It had been a long time. They were sweethearts at one time, before she met Michael. Bert thought that he loved her. She remembered one night when they almost ran away together. He had been her first love.

But then, along came Michael Walcott—and no other man compared. Still, Bert had been kind and romantic.

They were just children! She almost laughed. She was only one year older when she married Michael. It would be interesting—seeing Bert again—and she wondered how much they each had changed.

"Katie, we better get you back to the cottage."

Katherine was a master at changing a subject, Kate noticed.

"John, we have so much to do—you know, girl things—and, tomorrow, if you or Mac—or the caterer—needs help, I'm definitely your woman."

John thanked her. Mac raised his eyebrows. Kate sighed.

"Mom's right. We better say 'goodnight'. Mom, I'll be right there. Maybe Mac would see you over to the cottage, while I speak to John a minute."

Mac got up to escort Katherine back to the cottage. He knew Kate wanted to be alone with John. If for no other reason, to talk about how this tiny, petite, "twister" was getting ready to run the show!

"Come on, Katherine. I'll walk you back to the cottage. You once lived there, I hear?"

As they left, Kate went over to where John was seated. She stood behind his chair and bent over, putting her arms around his neck. He caught one of her arms and kissed her wrist.

"Wow!" he said. "So that's Katherine Turner Walcott. She makes quite a first impression, Kate."

Kate burst into laughter.

"I couldn't have said it better," she laughed. "She does have a way of taking over, doesn't she?"

"Well, in this case, it might be a good thing—if she doesn't drive you crazy doing it. I want you to be able to relax, Kate. Give her a list of 'to-dos' and let her at it tomorrow! She'll be happy—and you won't have nearly as much to think about."

"I knew if anyone could put a good spin on things, it would be you, Mr. Cabe." Kate leaned over and kissed him on the side of his cheek.

"I love you, Miss Walcott," he smiled.

"I love you more, Mr. Cabe," she whispered.

Kate could not convince her mother that she still had to fix breakfast for the family the next morning.

"Nonsense!" Katherine snapped. "It's your Wedding Day—besides, you can't see the groom, and he isn't allowed to see the bride on his wedding day."

Kate grinned at her mother, "Mom, he isn't able to see me."

"But, you can see him. Now, stop—I'll go fix some breakfast. You, my darling daughter, are going to stay here and have a bubble bath. I'll bring you some coffee and toast. Don't worry, I'll check with the caterer. You know I'm good at planning things."

Kate remembered what John had said to her. She did have to admit that, as pushy as her mother was, she was good at details and she would take care of everything. She thought of Mac being forced to 'endure' her mother's bossiness, and she had to smile.

"Okay, Mom," she sighed, "you win. But, if the Stewarts and Matthew arrive, please send Alex and Sabrina out here—and Matthew too. I need to speak to them."

Her mother nodded to her, and left. Kate took in a deep breath, and headed for the bathroom. A bubble bath might be nice.

Chapter Eighteen

The Stewart family arrived at John's ranch about 11:00 a.m. Sabrina Stewart got out of the car, ran up the steps, and opened the front door. She walked into the Cabe house without knocking, and almost collided with Katherine Walcott, who was carrying a bowl of flowers into the living room.

"Oh, careful young lady. You almost got me," exclaimed Katherine.

"I'm sorry," replied Sabrina. "Uncle Johnny?"

The child yelled out, and then spied John Cabe. At that point, black curls, blue eyes and skipping feet bounced over to him, and she wrapped her arms around his legs.

"I'm here, Uncle Johnny," she exclaimed. "I'm so glad to see you."

John Cabe leaned down and swung the child up on his broad shoulders. He grinned, and then called out to Mac.

"Look who's here, Mac. If it isn't our Sabrina! How are you, doll?"

"Sabrina!"

Mac came over, and tugged at the child's toes.

"Where are your parents?"

"They're coming. They're just slow," the child whined. "It sure looks beautiful in here, Uncle Johnny."

Nicholas Stewart came in, carrying wedding gifts, suitcases, and toys. Katherine Walcott drew in her breath when he entered. He was not at all what she expected. Oh, he was handsome all right—tall, dark hair, good looking—but today, he looked like a—a 'Dad'!

"Hey, Buddy," he said, as he crossed the room to John, "sorry about Sabrina—she was so excited. You do know you're supposed to wait, Sabrina. Go and help your mother with that surprise, okay?"

"Okay, Daddy. I'm sorry I didn't wait."

The child turned to Katherine Walcott.

"I'm sorry I almost ran into you. My daddy didn't raise me like that."

The child's apology was evidently something she had heard her father say before. Katherine Walcott didn't know whether to laugh, or just accept it. She was smart, this five or six-year-old. She reminded her of Katie, at that age.

"It's all right, young lady. You just go help your Mother, okay?"

Katherine decided that the Stewarts must be *old* friends of John Cabe's. They certainly made themselves right at home!

Sabrina came back in, carrying a large wrapped gift. Following her, through the front door, was the most stunning woman Katherine had seen in a long time. She wore a light blue dress, with a loose fitting jacket, and shoes to match. Her blonde hair was tied back with some tiny flowers. So, this was Alexandra Stewart—Katherine went over to her, and introduced herself.

"Mrs. Stewart? I'm Katherine Walcott, Katie's mother."

"I'm so pleased to meet you, Katherine," Alex answered.

So, this is Kate's mother. Alexandra formed an opinion almost as fast as she had fallen in love with Nick. Katherine Walcott took charge, she decided, but Alex also saw vulnerability in her that the men in the room may have missed.

If Alexandra had been given one thing in her walk with the Lord, it was discernment. She looked right into Katherine Walcott's soul, and saw so much pain there that she almost gasped.

"So, Mrs. Walcott, where is Kate? I want to see her before the wedding."

Katherine led Alex Stewart to the cottage out back.

"I told her that it was bad luck to see the groom on her wedding day. I've had to take care of the wedding details, while she relaxes a little, and gets dressed. I'm glad you're here Alexandra. Maybe you can talk to her. She's a nervous wreck."

"I'd be glad to speak to her, and I'll be happy to help you with anything, Katherine."

Katherine sensed that Alex Stewart could calm down anyone—even her. She knocked on the cottage door, and told her that she would leave her alone with Kate.

"I think she wants to see you alone, Alexandra."

With that, Katherine Walcott left.

Alex entered the cottage. The sunlight was streaming in the windows. When she stayed before, she hadn't noticed the cottage. It was darling—a place she might have picked out for herself, before she married Nicholas.

"Kate?" she called out.

Alexandra hoped that Kate wasn't quite as frantic as her mother made her out to be.

"Kate? It's Alex. Are you in here?"

Kate Walcott appeared from the bathroom in a terry robe, and with a towel wrapped around her hair.

"Alexandra. I'm so glad that you're here."

Kate ran over and hugged Alex. She didn't seem the slightest bit "nervous" to Alex, as her mother had suggested. Instead, Alexandra saw a very relaxed young woman, and she was amazed when she looked at Kate's face. There were *no scars—none!* Alexandra remembered the swelling, and the redness, that she had seen in the hospital. What had happened?

"Kate, you look wonderful."

"Oh, Alex, thanks. I have to get my hair dry and get dressed, but I have plenty of time. Please, sit down. I have tea. Would you like some?"

Alexandra sat. Was this the same young woman that she had seen in the hospital? She was so frantic back then. This woman—Alex saw that Kate Walcott was totally healed! She bore no scars outside, and it seemed that she was healed on the inside, too. This must have been the "miracle" that Dr. Martin and Maureen knew would happen.

"Alex, I know this has happened so fast, but I wanted to talk to you.

I know that you're John's best friend. He loves you so much. I just wanted to let you know—I really love him, Alexandra. I've never loved anyone so much. I believe God put him in my life—and me in his. Does that make sense?"

Alexandra Stewart gave Kate a hug.

"It makes perfect sense, Kate. Nothing has made more sense."

"I guess you met my Mom, huh?"

"Just now. I'm glad that she's come. Have you two made up?"

"We have. I know she can be a pain. She likes to take charge. But John told me to 'let her do just that'. So, I did. You know, it's not half-bad. I've had the entire morning to myself. It's been great!

Alex smiled. She had always liked Kate, even when Nick had doubts about her.

"Well, how can I help? Does your dress need pressing? Or, do you want me to help you with your hair? I'll do anything, Kate."

Kate smiled at her. Alexandra had been her friend when she had no friends.

"Alex, if you'll just sit with me, and help me with my makeup and hair, that will be great! I have to show you my dress. Where's Sabrina? Matthew will be here soon, and he's really missed her."

"How is Matthew? We've all thought about him. He's such a great kid!"

"He's just wonderful, Alex. He's so excited about the wedding. He wants to be a part of our family so much, Alex. I've prayed and prayed that it will work out. It just has to—for John's sake."

Alex could hear the pain in Kate's voice. Thinking of Matthew not being able to live with them must tug at her heart. She knew that Kate loved Matthew as much as John did. They just had to get him.

"Don't worry, Kate," Alexandra said, as she touched Kate's shoulder. "Your Matthew will come here and he'll be able to stay. I just know it. He loves you and John."

"Sometimes that's not enough," said Kate. "Sometimes you have to have friends in high places. That's one reason Judge Nichols is marrying us, Alex. He has to see our home. Oh, Alex—I'm so nervous about him. He knows my mother. They went to school together. Can you believe that?"

"John told us some of it. I can't believe how it's worked out, Kate. Can you? If you don't believe in miracles, just look back a few weeks!"

"I know, Alex—believe me, I know."
"Come on, let's see that dress."

Matthew Clark arrived with a children's worker from the hospital. He jumped from the van, and ran up the steps of the ranch house.

"Yeller! I told you I'd be back. Hi, fellow."

Matthew had stopped to see his friend. The yellow cat was in his favorite spot—curled up on the rocker, on the front porch. Matthew picked up the cat, and carried him inside.

"Sabrina!" he yelled.

Sabrina Stewart ran over to her friend, and gave him a hug. She almost knocked Yeller from Matthew's arms.

"What's that cat doing in here?"

It was Kate's mother.

"I don't think she likes him, Matthew. You'd better take him outside," said Sabrina.

"Matthew?"

It was John Cabe.

"Come over here, son—you and *Yeller* come over here."

Matthew grinned at Sabrina, and both he and the cat went over to see his very best friend—John.

"John—I'm here. I'm back. Hi, Mr. Stewart—Boy, am I glad to see you and Sabrina again!"

Nick Stewart went over and hugged the boy. The cat didn't move. He had snuggled up, completely content, in Matthew's arms.

"Looks like you've made another friend, Matthew. Hi, Yeller— you old cat, you."

Nick Stewart scratched the cat's ears.

Katherine Walcott was totally confused. It seemed as if she had tried to "shoo" away a welcome guest. She would just have to cope.

"Where's your mother, Sabrina? Isn't she coming?"

"She's in the cottage, Matthew."

John Cabe interrupted them.

"You go tell Mrs. Stewart that I'm feeling very ignored. She didn't even say 'boo' to me before she went out to see Kate."

John wanted to talk to Alexandra alone, but he wasn't quite certain how he'd manage that, with this crowd of onlookers.

"I'll go tell her, Uncle Johnny. Come on, Matthew."

Sabrina had the boy's hand, and led him and the cat, out the back door.

"See, Nick—I told you she'd have that child eating out of her hand," grinned John.

Both of them laughed. John could just about see Sabrina leading Matthew around, and he could see Matthew liking every minute of it.

"You were right, John," answered Nick. "She calls him 'her Matthew,' and she talks about him every day. John, I guess we should go and get you ready. This *is* your Wedding Day—remember?"

"I remember. I guess I could use some of that Nick Stewart charm right now. Will you help me?"

"It would be my pleasure, Bud."

"And, Nick?"

"Yes, John?"

"Could you make sure that I get to talk to Alexandra before the ceremony?"

"I can do that. Now, let's go see what you're wearing."

The two of them left the room. Katherine Walcott turned to Mac, motioning for him to follow her. She still had to check on the buffet. Mac grinned at her, as he went into the kitchen. Katherine still had a lot to learn from his "boys."

"Kate, it's beautiful—you look so beautiful."

Alexandra Stewart stood back and admired her own handiwork. She had pulled Kate's hair up in back, but combed soft tendrils down each side of her face and along her neckline in the back. She framed Kate's face further with a soft bang, and tied in some lilacs and baby's breath.

Kate wore simple pearl and silver earrings. The seed pearls on the dress encircled her neck.

The dress...Alex wondered...*How had Kate found that dress, here in Clarksville? It would stand up to any Designer Dress in New York City. The flowers look like a watercolor palette, complimenting Kate's auburn hair and her fair features. She is simply beautiful.*

"Here, you need something 'borrowed'."

Alex handed Kate her bracelet. It was sterling, and it matched the pearl and silver earrings.

"Oh, Alex, thank you. I have my mother's handkerchief. That's 'old'. The dress and shoes are new. I won't tell you where my 'something blue' is," she smiled.

"Kate, you look absolutely wonderful. Your face—"

Kate quickly put her hand up to the right side of her face.

"Do the scars show too much, Alex?"

"Kate—what scars? You don't have any scars!"

Alexandra was stunned that Kate thought her burn scars were still there.

She watched, as Kate felt her face. She had seen the scars earlier. Then, Alexandra did her makeup. When she looked into the mirror— she thought it was just the makeup.

"Alex? What do you mean? The scars were there this morning. I'm not crazy. They were there. I just thought that you were a master at doing makeup."

Alex grabbed the mirror.

"Look! Feel your face, Kate. There are no scars. Kate, you've been healed. God has healed you totally!"

Alexandra and Kate both realized that they had just experienced God's miracle—together.

"Oh, Alex, how? I mean—why? Why now?"

Alexandra wondered if she had the total answer. She tried to say something that made sense to Kate.

"I believe you've forgiven yourself, Kate. You've forgiven your mother. You love John and Matthew. There's not a trace of the person that I saw in the hospital. That young woman was so afraid—and she was so angry with herself. That person was in so much pain. I think you may have even forgiven 'him', Kate—your stepfather. Am I right?"

Kate had tears in her eyes, as she nodded "yes" to Alex.

"Is forgiveness the key, Alex?"

"I believe it is, Kate."

"I'm ruining my makeup," she said, tears streaming down her cheeks.

"Then, they'll only see your beautiful face, Kate."

Alex hugged her again. She remembered what had happened to Nicholas and to her, when Nick forgave himself, and they had found each other! Then, she remembered the angels—and Alex smiled. She remembered—all of it, just as Nick had! They were real—she knew it, and now *she remembered them!*

"Let me go inside, Kate, and see if that Judge has arrived. Do you want me to send Mac in to you? He is giving you away, isn't he?"

"Yes. He's been so good to me, Alex. He's so much like a father to John."

Alex remembered her own wedding. Mac had given her away too. She loved him so much.

"I'll send him in…and your mother?"

"Tell my mom I'm ready, and that I'll see her when I walk down the aisle."

Alex smiled, and kissed Kate on her cheek. As she left, she ran into Matthew and Sabrina on her way out the door.

"Mama? Uncle Johnny says you ignored him. He wants to talk to you."

"Matthew—Sabrina—Would you like to see the bride before she gets married?"

"Oh, yes, Mama. Can we?"

"She asked to see both of you. I think it's all right. Just don't stay too long. You both need to come and sit with Katherine and me when you've done that, Okay?"

The two children peeked inside and then went into Kate.

"Oooh," whispered Sabrina.

"Kate, you look so beautiful," said Matthew.

Kate gathered them up in her arms. She was so full of joy.

"Kate?" asked Sabrina, "You look just like my angel. She's the angel that I saw, Matthew. It was Kate."

Matthew rolled his eyes, but when he looked up at Kate, she *did* look like an angel to him, too.

Chapter Nineteen

Judge Nichols drove his SUV up the gravel road to the Cabe Ranch. He parked behind several cars and walked up the drive. The ranch was well maintained. John Cabe had managed to take good care of it, despite his condition.

He knew that Katie would want his decision regarding Matthew as quickly as possible, even tonight—and he knew that it would take longer. It would be hard for her to wait. Kate had little patience, and in that respect seemed so much like her mother.

His hands began to sweat as he thought about seeing Katherine again. He had loved her so much once. The woman he saw the last time that she was in town was nothing like the girl he once loved. She had grown stiff, tense, and cold, after Michael's death. He could not believe that she had remarried.

Tolbert couldn't stand her new husband, although he had only met him one time. He was so unlike Michael. Something must have happened in their relationship. A few weeks ago, he signed her divorce papers, and she took back the name of Walcott again.

He rang the doorbell, hearing voices and laughter inside.

Katherine Spencer Walcott answered the door.

"Bert?" she questioned.

"Hello, Katherine," he answered.

She was still beautiful. The coldness he saw before was now replaced with a sadness that he recognized. She was lonely too, he thought. She would never want anyone to know that, especially not him.

"Come in, Bert."

She stepped to one side.

"Judge Nichols?"

John Cabe stepped out from his bedroom and walked toward the door. Tolbert Nichols was surprised how well he maneuvered through the room.

"Mr. Cabe? How are you, Sir?"

The judge admired John Cabe. He also saw another figure come through the door—Nicholas Stewart. He recognized him from his films, of course, but Matthew had spoken of him, too. He was Matthew's friend. He looked around for the boy, but didn't see him.

"I'd like you to meet my guests, Judge Nichols."

John introduced the Judge to Nick, to Mac, and last, to Katherine.

"Oh, I forgot. You two have already met."

Tolbert Nichols smiled at Katherine, and she smiled back. He had changed some. His hair was grayer, but he was still a handsome man. Katherine showed him to a seat, as Alexandra Stewart came inside.

"Alexandra, this is Judge Nichols," said Nick Stewart, "Judge, this is my wife."

The Judge stood back up.

"Mrs. Stewart, I can't tell you what an honor this is."

Nick smiled. When Alex entered a room, she still stopped time. He put his arm around her, glad that she was his.

"Mac, Kate's ready," said Alexandra. "When you go out there, send those children back inside, so that we can all go out together."

"I'll do it. Just give me a signal whenever you're ready."

"Alexandra? John wants to talk to you before the vows. You can use his study."

Nick Stewart was suddenly somber. He wouldn't turn his wife over to anyone—except his best friend, and hers. He knew that John needed to speak to her, and he guessed why.

"John, I haven't even spoken to you," Alex said, as she entered the study. "I'm so sorry. I've been dolling up your Kate, not that she needs it. She looks absolutely beautiful."

"She is, Alex. She is beautiful."

When she heard him say it, Alexandra knew that her friend had found his own true love. She went over to him, and hugged him.

"Well, beautiful," John began, "I'm afraid I've got another woman in my life."

He smiled, and Alex touched his face.

"I know, John. The thing is, that I really like her. We've become good friends—your Kate and I."

John put his arms around Alexandra. They meant so much to each other—Alexandra, Nick, and Mac. He didn't think he would ever feel as deeply for a woman, as he did for Alexandra. She was his "hero," his "sister" that he never had, and his very best friend. Other than Nick, there was always an indescribable bond between them.

"I love you, Alex," he said.

"I know." She was crying.

No one could explain this. Alex was so in love with Nicholas. He was her soul mate. She loved him more than life, itself. But, John—Johnny was her best friend, and he was like the brother she never had. She could share anything with him.

"Alex?" he said, as he lifted her chin.

"I'm so sorry, John. I'm so happy for you. I don't know why I'm crying."

"I do. Our relationship is changing and it's scaring you. Please don't cry, Alexandra."

"You'll have Kate to talk to now, Johnny. She will share everything with you. That's as it should be."

"And, *you* won't matter anymore? Is that what you think, Alex?"

"Oh, John, it sounds terrible, like I'm jealous—I'm not. You have to know that. I love Kate. I just want to be able to call my friend, when I need him—when I can't talk to anyone else—when Nick's on location—or Mac's gone. There's always been you, John. I'll miss that. It's so selfish of me."

She couldn't go on. Alexandra loved what Kate had done for John—she was so right for him.

"You can always call us, Alex. Only now, you'll have two of us—

we'll always be there for you—Kate and I—just as you and Nick have always been there for me. I love you both, the way you've loved me. I had to let you know that. Please don't give up on our friendship, Alexandra."

"Never, John. We're family. Now, we have two more joining us—Kate and Matthew."

Neither of them could explain. Not many people had a friend who would give up their life for you. They did—and they knew it.

"We better get you out there, John Cabe. They'll think that I kidnapped you."

She wiped her eyes with a tissue, straightened John's tie, and his boutonniere.

"You have a wedding to go to, Mr. Cabe."

John kissed her cheek, and then gave him her arm. When they got back into the living room, Nick was waiting for them. He smiled at both of them, and Alex walked over beside him.

"Hey, Love," he said, taking her arm.

She looked into Nicholas' eyes, and felt as she did the very first time she saw him. She fell in love all over again.

It turned out to be a beautiful afternoon. The garden was filled with roses, and the fragrance of the lilacs and honeysuckle filled the air. John took his place near the Judge, while Nick Stewart stood next to him as his best man. Alex sat with Katherine. Sabrina and Matthew were sitting next to Alex. Mac walked Kate outside, through the flowers, and down the path to her future husband.

Just as Alex and Katherine had seen Kate's transformation, so did Nicholas Stewart. There was an audible intake of 'breath' from him, as Kate walked through the garden and into the sunshine. Her skin was flawless. The sun hit her hair and it shined like the picture that Nick Stewart saw in the hospital. She looked exactly like the woman that John described to him as "Maureen"—and *exactly* like the angel he had seen in the painting!

Nick couldn't believe what he was seeing. The scars on Kate's face had completely disappeared. He wondered what had happened to her?

Kate Walcott smiled, as she walked into the sunshine to John.

"John?" she asked, as she moved next to him. "I'm here, John. I'm here—right beside you."

John Cabe grabbed her hand, and held on.

The reception for John and Kate went perfectly, just as her mother planned. The bride and groom cut their cake, and the punch was served. Adults talked, and children played—and John and Kate Cabe had their first dance, as a married couple.

"I promise you can take the lead, darling—always," Kate whispered to him.

John smiled, as he remembered their first dance. He pulled her close to him, and kissed her.

"You make it very easy, Kate. I love you."

Tolbert Nichols watched Matthew, as he looked at the new bride and groom. The child was smiling. When he had spoken to Matthew, they were all that he could talk about. How could he refuse the child's wishes to be a part of this family? He had made his decision. He walked over to Katherine Walcott then, and did something that few expected.

"Katherine? May I have a dance?"

She was so petite, and still very beautiful. She almost disappeared in his arms. Tolbert Nichols was remembering a first love—and so was Katherine.

Mac grinned at Matthew and Sabrina.

"Now, that's something," he said, as he watched them.

Nick took Alexandra's hand and led her to the floor. As she moved into him, she still managed to take his breath away.

"It's perfect, Nick. It's such a perfect ending," Alex sighed.

She glanced over at Katherine and Tolbert Nichols.

"Something's happening over there," she told Nicholas, "and it's a good thing, darling."

He looked over at the Judge and Katherine, then back at Alexandra. He smiled down at his wife. She was usually right about these things. He kissed her hair, and held her very close.

"It's a good thing here, too, darling."

John and Kate left the ranch with Matthew. They wanted to return him to the hospital personally, and say "Hello" to Dr. Martin and Maureen. The child was excited about the wedding, and he was talking a mile a minute.

Matthew asked John how soon Judge Nichols would let them know if he could live with them. John tried not to sound too discouraging, but he didn't want to get the boy's hopes up, if for some reason, it didn't happen.

"The Judge has his hearing set for next week," John told him. "I don't want you to be upset if we have to have another hearing, or if he decides something else, Matthew."

"But—John! He *has* to agree. He just has to. He seemed to have a real good time, tonight. Won't that help?"

Kate interjected, "It didn't hurt, Matthew. He likes you. I can tell. I think that he will listen to what you told him. He knows where you want to live."

"Then, why wouldn't he send me home with you?"

Kate didn't want to say out loud the one reason standing in their way—John's blindness. She felt terrible. What if Judge Nichols didn't let them have the boy? That just couldn't happen.

"I tell you what, Matthew. Tonight, before we go to bed, we all need to send a special prayer up. We need to ask that Judge Nichols really hears what we've all told him—that we love each other, and we want to be a family. I'm sure if we all do that, things will work out."

John Cabe was silent. He knew all too well that his disability might be standing in their way—even with Kate's help.

They got to the hospital, and while Kate found Dr. Martin, Matthew waited with John.

"John?"

"Yes, son?"

"I'm really glad you married Kate. She's really neat, you know?" John smiled.

"I know, Matthew. She really is 'neat'."

Kate returned with Dr. Martin.

"Well, I hear 'Congratulations' are in order! I couldn't wish for a happier ending for all of you. Matthew? It's way past your bedtime, I think."

"Aaaww, gee, Dr. Martin. It was a special day."

"I know it was. How about Kate taking you down to the Children's Unit and tucking you in? I'd like to speak to John."

"I'll be down to say good night too, son, after I talk to Dr. Martin."

"Come on, Matthew. Let's go."

"All the kids are going to think that you're their angel, Kate. You look just like her."

Kate glanced back at Dr. Martin. He was smiling, and nodded his head.

"Angel? You keep talking about her Matthew. Tell me about her," said Kate.

Dr. Martin grinned. Kate and John might be the only two who didn't know how much Kate Walcott resembled the Saint in his picture. Kate and Matthew walked down the hall, as Anthony Martin put his hand on John's shoulder.

"John, I'm so proud of you and of Kate. I want you to know that."

John wasn't sure what to say.

"Thanks, Dr. Martin. I was hoping that Maureen would be here, too. We wanted her to know, but I guess she's off tonight, huh?"

"She's not in the hospital, but I'll be sure to let her know that you and Kate dropped by. She's going to be so happy for you both. John? You do love Kate, don't you? It's not just for Matthew that you two did this, is it?"

"Never. I love Kate. She did move the wedding up, but that was all right with me. I never loved anyone as much as her, Doctor Martin."

"Good. Now, you be patient with that young lady. She's headstrong, as I'm sure you've found out. She's had so much to deal with, John. She has had to forgive so much, hasn't she?"

John wasn't certain how much Kate had told Dr. Martin, but suspected he knew a lot.

"Yes, she has. She is so much better, though."

"She is, you're right. She's in love. You two are right for each other. Take care of each other, John."

Kate came back from the Children's Unit and walked up to John and Anthony Martin.

"Matthew wants you to tuck him in too, John."

"Guess I'd better do that then."

"Do you need me to walk down there with you?"

"No, I remember the way—even how many steps."

As he slowly started down the hall, Kate turned back to Dr. Martin.

"Why, Dr. Martin? Why?" she asked.

"Why?" The question surprised him, "What do you want to know, Kate?"

"You must have noticed. My scars are totally gone. I figured if anyone knew why, it would be you."

"You are direct, aren't you Kate?"

"I've never been good at playing games, Dr. Martin. Alex Stewart told me that she thought it was because I had forgiven my stepfather, and myself. She also told me loving John was a big part of it, too."

"Alexandra—she has been given a gift, all right. She sounds right on cue, Kate."

"Then, tell me," she paused, seeking the right words, "Why isn't John healed? He's done so much more than I. I would take the scars back, right now, if it would bring his sight back. Why couldn't it have been him who was healed, and not me?"

Anthony Martin was overwhelmed at her love for John. She meant it. She was willing to go through life scarred, if it meant his sight could be restored.

"Kate, that's the most unselfish thing I've ever heard..."

"Unselfish? No, Dr. Martin. I will always have to live with what I've done, but why John? He's the kindest, most unselfish man I've ever met. Please give me some hope. Will he ever be able to see? Will he ever see *me*?"

He couldn't answer her. He didn't know why John's sight hadn't been returned to him. He knew Kate would have to be patient for one more miracle, but this would be hard for her.

"Kate, I don't have an answer. We just have to trust that there's a reason. I've always thought that John would get his sight back. I just don't know when.

She surprised him even more.

"Dr. Martin? Will you pray with me?"

Kate Walcott was asking him to pray with her. He smiled—now, there was a real miracle!

"Kate, I'd be happy to pray with you."

They bowed their heads, and Kate asked for John's healing, and for her patience. She asked that he know her love for him. Then, she asked that Matthew be able to come and live with them. Anthony Martin agreed with her in prayer, and he asked a special blessing on this family, and that they would weather and endure any problems.

As they finished, Dr. Anthony Martin saw the glow surround them. He prayed silently that she and John would be ready for what was going to happen to them.

John and Kate let the Stewarts stay with Mac, in John's ranch house, while Kate's mother spent the night in the cottage. Kate and John made reservations at the town's Lake Lodge, in a small cabin they rented for a week. They wanted to stay close by, and near the Hospital, in case Judge Nichol's decision was made earlier than expected.

Kate and John Cabe checked into the Lodge and were shown to their cabin. It was small and quiet—just off the lake. The manager unlocked the door for them, and Kate led John inside.

"Oh, John, it's beautiful. Here, I'll show you where everything is."

There wasn't much furniture to run into. There was a small kitchen and bath. The living room consisted of a sofa, chair, and a fireplace. The bedroom included a bed and a double dresser. It was rustic, but it was peaceful.

John didn't know why he started to have doubts about everything. He even began to feel slightly awkward.

What if Kate wasn't really ready for this? What if, after all of this, she only married me this fast to keep Matthew?

He sat down on the sofa, in front of the fireplace, trying to shrug off the doubts.

"Would you like a fire, Kate? It's a little chilly tonight. I thought I felt some wood already stacked over here."

"I'll start one," she answered. "You just relax. I'd love a fire."

She found the logs, put them in the fireplace and lit the kindling. John found the radio, and turned it to some music. They were alone once more, and it was as if he had lost his voice, and any sense of how to treat his new wife, along with it! He didn't know how to begin.

"John?"

"Yes, Kate?"

She sensed his hesitancy, and tried hard to relax too.

"The Lodge delivered a beautiful gift to us. There's a bowl of fresh strawberries, and a basket of fruit—I opt for coffee. How about some?"

He grinned, and breathed a sigh of relief.

"There's my Kate. Coffee sounds good. I've had enough food for tonight, haven't you?"

"Definitely. I'll put the coffee pot on, and then come and sit in front of the fire with you. Just get comfortable."

She said a quick prayer to calm down, as she waited for the small pot to perk. She poured two cups of black coffee, and sat down next to him.

"Here you go."

He took the cup, and her hand touched his. She let it linger on his fingers. He sat the cup down on the coffee table.

"This is nice," she said. "We can finally relax."

It was the furthest thing from what they were doing. Why was this so hard? Both of them started to say something at the same time, and John finally laughed.

"This is ridiculous. We don't have to be this nervous, do we? Mrs. Cabe, would you come and dance with me?"

"I'd love that, Mr. Cabe."

As they got up, he pulled her to him. Suddenly, Kate felt all of her anxiety leave, as she laid her head on his chest. They didn't need to dance. John touched her hair, ran his fingers over her face and down her throat, touching the neckline of her dress. Kate felt her pulse quicken.

"Your gown," he began, "is the softest thing I've ever touched. What does it look like, Kate? Describe it to me."

She forgot he couldn't see the colors of her dress. She wanted him to see it—to see her!

"It looks like the closest thing I could find to a spring garden, John. I wanted it to look like the garden we got married in. There are lilac colors in it, and there's a morning glory blue—and the soft green of a maple leaf in spring. It's like someone started a watercolor, and then let all of the colors run together."

He decided that she was a wonderful storyteller. He could almost see the dress when she described it to him. She would look wonderful in it, with her auburn hair. He touched her hair. It was so soft, and she had pulled it up in back.

He slowly pulled out the pins that held it, and let it fall to her shoulders. Kate trembled, as he wove his fingers through her hands and pulled her closer to him.

"Kate—oh, Kate. I do love you."

He found her face, tilted her chin up, and put his mouth on hers. She had never been kissed like that, so gently, and yet, with a passion they both felt. Their wedding had not taken place too fast—nor had it been too soon. It had taken place at *exactly* the right moment!

"I love you too, John," she whispered, "and, so very, very much."

As they walked into the bedroom they could now share, Kate glanced back at the fire in the fireplace. The embers exploded and glowed, much like their love had. Kate relaxed completely. At last, she was home with her true love!

Chapter Twenty

The Stewart family flew home the morning after the wedding. Alexandra apologized to Katherine, telling her that Sabrina had to get back to school. Although Katherine said that she was sorry they couldn't stay longer, she really didn't mind. She was having lunch today with Bert Nichols. He had asked her out, right after the wedding. She slipped into a new cream-colored shirt and a celery green suit. As she ran a comb though her short auburn hair, she went over to her jewelry box.

"Hmmm. What should I pick?"

Her hand went to the Jade bracelet and earrings.

"These should do nicely," she said. "Yes, he'll like these."

Taking one last look in the mirror, she turned, picked up her purse, and walked out the door. Mac Timmons told her that he would drive her into town. She hoped that Tolbert Nichols would drive her back.

She found Mac waiting for her on the front porch. She smiled at him, and walked with him to the waiting car.

"How many vehicles does Mr. Cabe own, Mac?"

Katherine saw the jeep and a truck. Kate and John had driven the

Buick into town. The car she stepped into was an older Cadillac.

"He's a little like me. He has a thing for cars—likes to fix them up and tinker with them. It's kind of a hobby, you know? I think he has six or seven cars. He lets the boys on the ranch use the SUV, and the truck—anytime that he doesn't need it. Of course, he's got his planes too."

"Big boys and their 'toys', Mac?" Katherine asked.

"More than a toy, Ms. Walcott. The airline company's his livelihood. I'm a partner, you know?"

She didn't know that, but she nodded to Mac.

"I like John."

"So does your daughter. They make a good team, Ms. Walcott."

Mac was surprised that Katherine Walcott admitted to liking someone. She seemed to have a lot of money, and leaned toward people who also had money. He could be wrong, but he didn't think so. She was so different from Kate. Maybe that was what Kate was running from, when she didn't want to return home.

Still, he had to admit that Katherine was pretty. She was a tiny woman, but made a powerful impact. It was evident to Mac, and everyone else, that she was used to getting her way. He was surprised that Judge Nichols knew her. If he wanted to see her again, it must have been pretty serious between them at one time. If it helped return Matthew to John and Kate, Mac was all for it. He drove her to the Court House and dropped her off.

"I'm here to see Tolbert Nichols," Katherine told the clerk.

"Your name?"

"I'm Katherine Walcott. I have an appointment."

"Oh, yes—Ms. Walcott—right this way."

The court clerk led her back to his chambers. Judge Tolbert Nichols rose, as she entered.

"Katherine," he smiled. "I'm so glad that you accepted my invitation."

He walked over and kissed her cheek.

"Bert," she smiled. "We have a lot of catching up to do, don't we?"

"It's been years since anyone called me 'Bert'," he laughed.

She looked around the office.

"It's very nice, Bert," she told him. "How long has it been since they elected you?"

"Just before Janie died," he said, "—about three years ago."

"I'm sorry about Jane. I really liked her. So did Michael."

"—and you, Katherine? How are you doing?"

He sounds interested, she thought. She could never tell him about what had happened between her ex-husband and Katie. Her eyes clouded when she thought about it. Bert Nichols already knew too much about her. He was the attorney in her own rape case, so many years back.

"I've been fine. I've been worried about Katie, with the wreck and all—but, it looks as if she's doing fine. I really like her new husband. He seems a decent sort."

"Yes, John Cabe is a good man. He's something of a hero, you know. Before the accident and before he moved here, he worked for Nick Stewart. Of course, you know all of that."

"Yes, Katie told me a lot. She's very much in love, Tolbert."

"Katie," he said her name out loud, remembering Katherine's red-haired toddler.

"You two still resemble each other, Katherine."

"I'll take that as a compliment, Bert. Kate's turned into a lovely young woman. I'm very proud of her."

"You should be. Now, how about that lunch?"

Tolbert Nichols was determined that he was going to see Katherine Walcott for more than just lunch. He was fortunate to find her again and he didn't want to lose her.

Kate woke up to the smell of fresh coffee. When she looked over toward the kitchen, she saw John through the open bedroom door. He must have found everything that he needed, and was making coffee for them. She smelled something else that smelled almost like cookies baking.

"What is that, darling?" she said, getting up from the bed, and heading to the kitchen. "Something smells just wonderful."

John smiled, and turned her way.

"Fresh cinnamon rolls," he grinned. "Well—almost fresh. The hotel delivered them while you were still sleeping. I just put them in the oven to warm."

"Sounds wonderful," she yawned. "Sorry, dear, late night..."

He smiled at her.

"Up late, huh? Enjoy your evening?" he teased.

"Very much."

She walked over to him, and put her arms around his waist.

"I could get used to this," he said, as she kissed the back of his neck. "Hey, that's not fair," he said, as she moved her lips directly behind his ear.

"I remember someone saying they don't play fair when they want something—wasn't that *you?*"

"Hmmm—sounds like something I may have said a long—long time ago."

She poured two cups of the steaming coffee, and handed one to him.

"I'll get those rolls out of the oven now. They smell great! Go sit down, John. You've done the hard part. I'll bring them to the table."

Kate took the potholder, and removed the warm pastries from the oven. Getting down three plates, she put the rolls on one of them, and then took them over to where John was waiting for her.

"Here you go! Watch it, darling—they're hot!"

"Just like you, Beautiful!"

He enjoyed teasing her. It was light and fun, and it was something that they hadn't done enough of, recently.

Kate kissed him, remembering last night. He had been so gentle with her. She didn't know that it could be like that—not after the rape. She wasn't sure that she could ever be with a man, after that happened—but John had been her strength, her lifesaver. She loved him so much—now, more than ever.

"Mrs. Cabe, you're making me forget all about breakfast."

"Good. We need to let the rolls cool off, anyway."

John grinned. He was feeling almost like his old self again. Their night had been nothing short of indescribable. Kate Walcott Cabe had completely won his heart.

It was after 10:00 a.m. before John and Kate had breakfast. They sat across from each other—with Kate watching every move he made. John listened to her breathe, took in her scent, and reached for her hand. The touch of her made him alive. They were newlyweds—and they were in love with each other.

"John?"

"Yes, Beautiful?"

"Do you think we should call Mac, and see if Judge Nichols has phoned?"

"Let's wait until tomorrow, Kate. Today's our day—no phone—no TV—just you and me. I love you, Kate Walcott Cabe."

She got up from the table and walked over to him, putting her arms around his neck. She found it was difficult to breathe around him! Her heart pounded, and her knees got weak. She felt like a young girl, in love for the first time. She knew he was right. Today was theirs—*their day*.

Judge Nichols returned Katherine Walcott to the cottage, and walked her to the door.

"I hope we can see each other again, Katherine, before you fly back home."

"I'm leaving tomorrow, Bert. I have to get back to my business."

"Is there any possibility that you would let me visit you in Boston?"

Katherine was astonished that he would think about seeing her again. She wasn't certain if she were quite that interested in him. Still, he was a handsome man. Her friends in the Country Club could be quite taken with him, she supposed.

"I'd like that, Bert."

"I have a meeting near there, next month. I'll phone you. I'd like to take you out to dinner. I'll look forward to it, Katherine. This time, I have to talk you into going with me to a play or the Opera."

"Perhaps," she smiled. "Thank you, Bert. I had a nice time tonight. It was good—seeing you again."

He leaned forward, and kissed her on her forehead.

"Goodnight, Katherine."

Katherine Walcott wasn't sure if this would lead anywhere, but at least she could give it a chance.

"A Judge," she said under her breath, "...not too bad."

Katherine finished packing and got ready to leave the next morning. She had hoped that Katie or John would phone her, but realized they might forget about anyone, but each other. Mac took her suitcases to the car, and she wrote them a note. She left a check with the note. Her daughter deserved something nice. It would be her wedding gift to them. She left the note, and money on the small table in the foyer and left for the airport.

Kate and John phoned the ranch house that morning, to see if Mac had heard anything from the Court, but there was no answer. Finally, John phoned Kent Able, his foreman.

"Mac and Mrs. Walcott just left, John," Kent told him. "She's on her way to the airport today."

"Oh, I'm sure Kate wanted to tell her mother goodbye. I'll have her phone the airport. Maybe she can still catch her. Thanks, Kent."

John went into wake Kate. He stood by the bed a moment, and just listened to her breathing. She had slept well, last night. He hated to disturb her this morning, but knew that he had to wake her.

"Kate? I'm sorry to wake you up."

He leaned over the bed where she was sleeping, and then sat down on the edge of the bed.

"John? Is something wrong?"

"No, dear—I just wanted to let you know that Katherine's on her way to the airport. I thought you might be able to catch her, to say 'goodbye' before she left."

"Oh, I do need to speak to her—at least, say goodbye."

He handed her the phone and she dialed the airport. She asked that they page her mother and have her call their number.

"Thanks, darling. They're going to have her paged. She'll call us."

"Good. I'd hate to start out on her bad side. She's pretty ferocious, isn't she Kate?"

John was joking, as he said it, but he knew there was also a lot of truth to the statement. Katherine Walcott was no one to tangle with, especially if you didn't have to.

"See why I was afraid to tell her? At least, at first—I just found out that she has a softer side that she never lets anyone see, John. It hasn't been easy for her since Dad died. I understand her a bit more, now."

"I am glad for you, Kate," he said softly. "I'm glad that you found out what you did about your mother and your father—for your sake."

She moved over to the edge of the bed, where he was sitting.

"It made a world of difference, John. It was a miracle."

"I know."

He gathered her in his arms and held her, as she took a deep breath and leaned against his chest. She felt so safe. She could face anything with him.

Chapter Twenty-One

Judge Nichols signed the guardianship papers, and then phoned the Cabe household, and Children's Services. Matthew could go home with the Cabe family, as soon as they returned from their honeymoon. He smiled, as he wrote his signature in a broad, bold hand.

"A present for you Katherine—and for you, too, Katie and John," he said. "Maybe you'll remember what I just did, Katherine, when I come and visit you next month."

Mac Timmons wouldn't have disturbed the two young people for anything, but this was what they both had been waiting for. He picked up the phone and dialed the Lodge, where Kate and John Cabe were staying.

"John? Mac here. I have some wonderful news."

John Cabe yelled at Kate, and asked her to come to the phone.

"Here, darling—I'm going to let Mac tell you what he just told me."

He had such a large smile on his face, that she knew it had to be good news.

"Mac?" Kate questioned.

Mac Timmons told her about the guardianship. All they had to do now was to go and sign the papers.

"Oh, Mac! Thank you—thank you so much. We'll go over to the Court House right away. This is the best present we could ever have had for our Wedding."

She hugged John, as she handed him the phone.

"Mac," John continued, "is the Judge going to be there today? Or, do we have to wait? He is? Good. Call him back and tell him you got in touch with us. We'll be over at the Court House as soon as we can get dressed and drive there. We don't want to wait another day!"

John hung up and grabbed Kate around her waist, swinging her up off the floor, until she was dizzy.

"Matthew can come home with us, Kate! He's coming home!"

They were both deliriously happy. Kate was laughing and crying all at the same time, and John was shouting loudly enough, that the people in the cabin next door could hear them.

"It's a wonderful day, Kate. Let's go get those papers signed and go pick up Matthew."

John and Kate Cabe cut their honeymoon short. They packed, drove to the Court House, and signed the guardianship papers. They thanked Tolbert Nichols, as he seemed to beam with pride.

"Is it okay if we pick up Matthew, now?" they asked.

"I should certainly think so. Good luck Mr. Cabe—Katie—and Congratulations!"

John and Kate left to go and pick up their child—their "Matthew."

Dr. Martin and Maureen had Matthew's clothing packed and ready. Children's Services phoned to let them know the Judge's decision, and that it was all right to release Matthew to Mr. and Mrs. John Cabe. Maureen smiled, as John and Kate arrived.

"Congratulations, you two!" she beamed. "We just heard. What a happy day for both of you. Oh, it's wonderful—Matthew is waiting for you. He can hardly stand it."

As Maureen hugged Kate, Kate Walcott felt a warmth go through her, that she felt once before, when she had been with Maureen.

"Maureen?" she asked

189

"Yes, dear?"

Maureen McConnell knew what she wanted to know.

"Was it you? Was it you who healed me?"

"No, dear Kate. It was you—and God—don't you know that? We just waited, and we prayed."

Kate looked over at John. He had heard her question, but didn't quite understand. He knew that when he felt Kate's face, he had not felt any sign of burns or scars—but it wasn't important to him. She was beautiful to him, regardless. Her soul and her spirit were what mattered to him. Now, he realized something miraculous must have happened.

"Maureen?"

"Yes, John—my dear friend—"

"Would you tell us about this place? It's called Saint's Hospital— I've always felt something special here—a peace I could never explain. You always told me that you would never lie to me, Maureen. Tell us."

Maureen looked over at Dr. Martin. He shook his head. They couldn't know, just yet. John and Kate Cabe had a final trial—a difficult test—one that he wished they didn't have to face. He came over, and put his arm around Kate and John.

"There's nothing else to say, John. We pray. That's all it is."

Maureen took in a deep breath. She had not been forced to lie to him. Dr. Martin had told him the truth—but not all of it. It was also evident, to both Maureen and Dr. Martin, that Nicholas and Alexandra Stewart had also kept their secret for them. They had not told the couple standing there—anything—just as they had promised.

"Now, then—don't you want to go get that little boy of yours?" Maureen asked them.

"You bet. We've been here too long, Kate. Let's go and get Matthew!"

They all but ran back to the Children's Unit. Maureen smiled at Dr. Martin, and he put his arm around her shoulder. They could hear Matthew all the way down the hall. He was going home—*home!*

Chapter Twenty-Two

The small family of three sang songs all the way back to the ranch. Even John tried to sing.

"John was right," Matthew whispered to Kate. "He really can't carry a tune."

But John sang anyway—and Matthew just sang louder, to cover up John's voice. Kate laughed at both of them, her voice lifting up, and out the window—all the way to the heavens, and to her Lord. She had to thank Him! She had a real family. Matthew and John had a family! How had this happened, other than God?

They drove into the driveway at John's ranch and saw 'Old Yeller' waiting on the porch, and Mac coming out the front door.

"Come in, come in here." He threw his arms around Matthew.

"Mac, I love you. I get to stay, Mac. I get to stay here!"

"I know, boy. We wouldn't have it any other way!"

"Yeller—see, I'm back boy. I told you I'd come back. My angel told me so!"

Kate nudged John.

"He's talking about his angel again, John. I think he really has one."

"I know he does. Sabrina talked about her, too."

"I know someone's watched over us. Why not angels?"

"Why not, indeed?"

"Come on, you three. Get the cat, and come inside. I have a wonderful lunch, Matthew—one of your favorites—hot dogs!"

Kate laughed at them.

"Someday, Matthew, we'll have to fix you something healthy."

"It's healthy, Kate. I made a macaroni and cheese casserole to go with them, and even some peas and carrots."

"Wow, Mac. I may just give up fixing meals. You outdid me."

She went over to him, kissed his cheek, and hugged him.

"She's a good one, John. You better keep her."

"I intend to, Mac. I definitely want to keep her—and Matthew—for the rest of my life."

Mac walked over to John, and took his hand, then hugged him.

"You've done good, Johnny. I love you—you *and* Kate, for what you've been able to do. That's a fine young man you saved, John. It was meant to be. I knew if from the first time that I saw the three of you together at the hospital."

"Let's eat, Mac," called Matthew.

"Okay boy," he said over his shoulder. "Hold your horses. I need to get the iced tea out."

John grinned. He loved the banter between them. He reached out for Kate. She had tears in her eyes that he couldn't see—but she saw his. She reached up, and kissed them.

"I love you, but I guess I've told you that once or twice in the past few days," she smiled.

"I'll never get tired of hearing it, Kate—never."

He leaned down, and kissed her back, and Kate felt her knees begin to give way, again.

"We better eat. We'll hurt Mac's feelings," she said.

"We'll eat—then play all day with Matthew—but later..." he whispered in her ear.

"Oh, I like that plan, Mr. Cabe. Can I count on that?" she smiled.

"You can count on it, Beautiful," he grinned.

He put his hand around her waist, as they walked to the kitchen, where Mac and Matthew were waiting.

Kate had never noticed how bright the morning sun was. It streamed through the kitchen window of the ranch, onto the counters, and the vase of daisies that graced the table. She had been up almost an hour, waiting for both Matthew and John to wake up. They had stayed up later than usual the night before.

It was nice—being home—showering and slipping into her own terry robe and slippers—letting her husband catch a few more winks, and making breakfast for a real family. She sipped her coffee at the counter, and then fed Yeller.

"It's you and me, Kid," she said, as she scratched behind the cat's ears. "They're all sleeping peacefully."

She removed the waffle iron from the cabinet, and then got down the ingredients that she needed.

"Waffles and sausages, Yeller," she told the cat. "It's a special day. Matthew is home. That may mean fewer scraps under the table for you, but I'd guess you don't mind. You kind of like him, huh?"

She walked over to the phone and called Mac, who was staying in the Cottage.

"Good Morning, Mac. Are you up? Good. I hate having coffee alone. Come on over. John and Matthew are still asleep."

She was smiling as she hung up the phone. The day couldn't be *more perfect*.

Mac Timmons picked up the newspaper from the porch, and walked over to the back door of the house. He tried to enter quietly, so that he wouldn't disturb the late sleepers. Mac grinned when he saw Kate.

"Morning!" he called out. "So your men are late getting up, huh?"

"They had a late night. Chinese checkers and hot chocolate nearly did both of them in," she laughed.

She poured Mac a cup of coffee, as he sat down on the kitchen barstool.

"Well, I'll keep you company until they decide to join us. Something smells good, Kate."

"Sausages and waffles—and I heated up the maple syrup. I'm going to have to wake up those sleepyheads pretty soon. Oh, good—you found the newspaper."

He passed the paper over to her, and she glanced at the Headlines, and then turned to her favorite section. Mac grinned, as he watched her turn to the Comic Section.

"That's my favorite part of the paper too," he smiled.

"I like to start the day right. Comics and a devotional seem to be the best way," she said, "and—my coffee, of course."

"Hey, what's going on?"

It was a small voice that was coming from the hallway.

"Matthew?" Kate asked. "Where are you?"

The child peeked around the corner.

"Hi. I wasn't sure if I should come out yet, or not?"

"Oh, sweetie. Of course you can come out here. Come and sit next to me and Uncle Mac, and I'll pour you some orange juice."

Matthew was dressed. Kate expected he would still be in his pajamas. He must have been awake longer than she thought.

"Did you sleep all right, Matthew?"

Kate handed him a glass of juice.

"Yeah. It was sure quiet, though. I kept waiting for a nurse or someone to come in and check on me."

Kate smiled.

"No more of that. I'm afraid I'll have to put Yeller in there with you tonight. He loves to snuggle with someone under the covers."

The boy sipped his juice, and smiled at her...his new "mom."

"I'd like that, Kate. Hi, Yeller."

The cat strolled over to where Matthew was sitting, and sat at his feet.

"I'll be. Look at that. The cat knows his name."

Mac couldn't get over the bond that seemed to exist between the boy and the cat. The cat ignored the rest of the family, except to eat and sleep.

"Matthew, go and wake up John. These sausages are going to shrink down to nothing if we don't eat soon."

She watched as the boy ran into their bedroom.

"That'll get him up—and he won't be grumpy with me, either."

Mac chuckled. He watched Kate, as she put the final items on the table. She was pretty in the morning—and he was sure that John would have loved seeing her without her makeup, with her hair tied up in a ponytail. He wished for that, more than anything. John needs to see Kate.

"Got any plans for the day, Katie?"

Mac had picked up her nickname from Kate's mother.

"I'm taking Matthew for a ride after breakfast. He loves that so much. John wants to phone Nick and Alex, and let them know what happened about Matthew."

"I wish John could ride with you, Katie. He loved it before—before the accident. He used it as a way to relax."

"I wish he could too. Maybe it's not impossible, Mac—if we stay on a trail. Maybe he could ride. I could watch him."

"I don't know. Maybe he'll be able to do that, later. He's still a little touchy about the things he used to be able to do and now…"

Mac stopped, as he saw her countenance darken. He had forgotten.

She's blaming herself again—and it's my fault.

"I'm sorry, Katie. I didn't mean that the way it sounded."

"It's okay, Mac. You're right. He used to be so active. I don't know how he's managed so far. He's doing so well. He's getting around so much better. He even walked down to the corral and stables with me the other day. He's amazing."

"Did I hear you just call your husband 'amazing', Mrs. Cabe?"

She turned to see John and Matthew coming from the bedroom.

"You just want to hear me say that again, don't you? John Cabe is amazing—there!"

She walked over to him, and kissed him.

"Aaww, mushy stuff," said Matthew.

John smiled and rumpled the child's hair.

"Get used to it, son," he laughed.

He smiled at Kate, and squeezed her hand.

"What smells so good?"

"Breakfast. And it's going to be shriveled and burned if we don't sit down."

The four of them gathered at the kitchen table.

"Grace!" said Matthew.

"Uh, what?" said Mac.

"Somebody hurry up and say grace, so that we can eat," the child said impatiently.

"Okay, how about you, Matthew?" asked John.

"Oh—okay."

Matthew bowed his head, and held his hands to either side. John took one, and Kate took the other, then she reached for Mac.

"Dear God, we're here. I sure thank you for my new home, and for my new family. Thanks for Yeller, too. Let Kate know that she's a really good cook, and let John know he's my best friend. Oh, I can't wait for the rest of the day! Amen."

Kate glanced at John and Mac. They were both smiling.

"That's a good prayer, Matthew," said Mac. "I couldn't have said it better, myself."

The breakfast was a "hit" for Kate. The men ate everything that she had fixed. She started the dishes, while John and Mac made their plans for the day. Matthew went to clean his room, so he could go riding.

"Maureen's coming out sometime this morning," said John. "She wants to check me out, I guess, and she wants to see Matthew. I guess I'll call Nick and Alex while you and Matthew are riding, Kate. Then, Mac and I'll wait for Maureen."

"That sounds good. We shouldn't be too long. I just want Matthew to see how much that colt's grown too."

She dried the dishes, and looked out the window. The grass was so green, and it seemed to her that every flower in the garden was blooming.

She went over and kissed her new husband.

"I'd better get changed," she said. "That child's *not* the most patient person in the world."

"Hmmm," John laughed, "reminds me of another family member that I know."

Kate punched his shoulder, and then went to get dressed.

"I'm going to go and get dressed too, Mac. Sorry I slept so late. She should have awakened me."

He joined Kate in the bedroom. She had slipped into a pink shirt and her jeans, and she was trying to find her boots.

"I don't know where I put my riding boots, John. What in the world...?"

"I think they're still in the cottage, Babe. Do you want Mac to run out and get them?"

"Oh no—I'll run out there. I'm almost ready. Tell Maureen we'll be

196

back soon."

Kate yelled for Matthew, and went out the back door to retrieve her boots from the cottage.

While Kate was in the cottage, putting on her riding boots, she thought she heard something—a strange sound. She couldn't tell exactly where was it coming from. She walked outside, and listened. Then, she heard the horse's whinny—and she knew that something was wrong.

She headed around the house, and across to the stables. It was Duke! She recognized his whinny, and she could hear him kicking the stall.

"What the—?"

Kate suddenly had a terrible fear invade her senses.

"Matthew?"

She began to run as fast as she could, toward the stable, crying out for the child. Could he have gone on without her?

"Matthew! Answer me!"

She began to panic, when she heard a faint noise inside the stable. It was Matthew's voice that was calling out to her.

"Kate? Kate! Help me—please!"

"Oh, God—No! Don't let him be in the stables. Protect him, God."

She flew into the stable, and stopped dead at the first stall. She froze!

"Matthew? Be still—stand totally still..."

The horse's hooves were flailing wildly. Matthew was barely inside of the stall. The horse hadn't reached him yet, and the gate to the stall was partially open. Then, Kate saw why Matthew had tried to enter. In the corner of the stall was a ball of yellow fluff.

"Yeller," she whispered.

"I'm sorry, Kate."

The child started to cry. The cat just lay there. She didn't know if he was dead or alive. The horse was frantic, now. He came toward Matthew. His nostrils snorted, making him appear as fierce and frightened as he had been the first time they saw him. Matthew ducked, and Kate went in, getting between the child and the horse.

"Go!" she yelled at Matthew.

She opened the gate wider, and Matthew slipped under her arm and out of the stall.

"Run, Matthew—run to the house! Tell them I need help."

Kate tried to reach the horse's halter, but she missed. The horse's front hoof hit her in the chest—and then her stomach. It knocked the breath from her.

"Duke, no." She was gasping for air.

Kate held her stomach, and fell back against the gate, closing it completely.

"Easy, boy—I know you're afraid."

She stumbled, but reached up, and opened the stall door again, this time, wider—to let him outside. The horse just stood there, looking down at her. Then, he whinnied, and started toward her again. Kate saw the whip hanging on the wall just to one side of the horse. She *had to reach it!* If she could just get to it, she could get the horse out of the stable.

She looked down at Yeller. He wasn't moving. If she could get to him...and she edged to the side of the stall, toward the whip...

John Cabe heard the noise. It was as if every hair on the back of his neck stood up, and he knew something was wrong. It was Matthew or Kate! He walked to the front door and listened, and then he heard the horse, and he heard the boy calling out. Last, he heard her—Kate's cries!

It was coming from the direction of the stables. John knew he had to reach them. He started down the front porch steps, and had gotten about halfway down the path from the house, when Matthew ran into him, almost knocking him down. The child began yanking John's hand and yelling at him.

"Matthew, what's wrong? Where's Kate?"

The boy was sobbing. He tried to talk.

"I'm sorry—Yeller, I tried to get to Yeller. The horse, John—the horse kicked him and then I tried to get him. Kate's there, John. She's in the stall—with Duke!"

The color drained from John's face, as he ran toward the noise. It didn't matter that he couldn't see. He had to get to her.

"Matthew—get Mac!" he yelled back at the child.

The child turned, and ran toward the house.

"God, please let me find her. Please! Show me your path. Oh, Lord, help me *see* where she is."

John stumbled over something in the path, but got up and kept going. All he could think of was Kate. He had to reach her—before the horse got to her.

It seemed like forever that he ran—then, right in front of him he thought he saw a light. First, it was dim, barely visible—then, more like a small flashlight—and then, the brightest light that he had ever seen! He was unable to look directly at it. He put his hand in front of his eyes. He thought he saw someone—a figure at the end of the light. Was it his Kate? Was he seeing Kate? He ran toward it...toward the light!

Kate tried to get to the whip again, as she saw the fire in the horse's eyes. She reached up to get it, and he kicked her again. This time, she fell, near the cat.

"No, Duke," she whispered.

The hooves hit her arms and her head. The pounding wouldn't stop.

"Please, God, help us," she prayed.

She found Yeller's ears, and covered him with her hands. The darkness enveloped her...

John Cabe heard the horse, as he entered the stable. He realized he could see light and dark—not clearly, but he could *see!*

*The very first thing that he saw clearly, when he entered, was Kate! She had fallen right below the horse...*The horse turned, when John entered. John Cabe didn't think of himself. He had to get to Kate.

He went inside the stall, and reached for the whip. The horse turned to him, ready to rear back, when John caught his flanks with the whip. He managed to open the gate as wide as he could, and turn the horse, using the whip over the horse's head—to guide him—outside the stall.

The horse flew from the stall, as John closed the gate and locked it. Until Mac could get here, there was nothing more he could do. He could hear the horse running the length of the stable.

"He has to go outside, Lord. Please let the other stable door be open."

John heard the horse's hooves keep going.

"Thank you, God."

John knelt down, pulling his wife to him. There was blood spattered everywhere.

"Kate? Oh, Kate, please talk to me!"

John Cabe sobbed, as he rocked her, and then, he saw Yeller, under her hand. Was she trying to protect him too? John realized that she had saved Matthew's life, but at what cost?

"Please, God—don't let her die. You can't let her die—not now!"

Maureen watched him, as he ran to his Kate. She could only light his way. Then, in this final act of courage and love, he *would* regain his sight, but she hated what he would find—what he had to see first. She prayed to heaven, and to her God, that he would find her in time.

Mac was on the phone with Nicholas Stewart, when Matthew came running into the house. Mac saw John run out of the house, just before the child came in. When he saw Matthew, he knew something was terribly wrong.

"My God, Nick, I don't know what's happening. Pray, Nick. Pray! Something bad has happened here."

Mac dropped the phone, and ran over to the boy.

Nick Stewart felt it to his very core, even at the other end of the phone line. He dropped to his knees, and prayed against an unknown evil that was endangering his friends!

After Matthew told Mac what happened, Mac grabbed his cell phone and ran with the child—down to the stables, where Mac found John kneeling—over Kate's body, and holding her head. He saw blood all around them.

"My God! Katie!"

Matthew stood behind Mac, trembling.

"Is she going to die, John? Please say she's okay."

"Call an ambulance, Mac. Kate? Can you hear me at all?"

Mac had his cell phone out, and had already begun to phone for an ambulance. There was so much blood. He knew that Kate was hurt bad. Then, Mac saw the cat, and he realized what must have happened.

"I'll call the vet, too, Matthew. Try not to worry. We'll get help."

Matthew was crying, as John turned to see the child. It was the first time that he had actually seen Matthew—his Matthew—his son. The child was heart-broken. In that instant, John Cabe wished that he wasn't able to see—first Kate, then Matthew—even Yeller. It was too much.

"Get him out of here, Mac."

"John? We need to stay."

Mac looked at John—at John's tears—at his eyes, looking right at Mac.

"John? Can you see us?"

John Cabe's eyes were filled with tears. He nodded to Mac, and then fell to the floor of the stall, beside his wife.

"Dear God? Please—please help them. Please help my family."

It was Matthew's voice. He was pleading for the life of Kate—and for John to forgive him—and for Yeller to live. The child went over, and knelt beside John. He lifted his small chubby hands together and up to heaven, while Mac wept openly, and while John put his arms around the boy, pulling him close to him.

"She'll be all right, son. She has to be."

John Cabe loved this child, but he never felt so helpless in his entire life.

The ambulance and the vet arrived simultaneously. John got in with Kate, and began the drive back to Saint's Hospital.

The boy and Mac waited in the horse stall, as the vet knelt over the animal's small body.

"He's still breathing," the vet said.

Matthew buried his head in Mac's coat and sobbed.

"I've got to get him to our hospital. He's pretty tough, Matthew. Try not to worry. I'll call you if anything changes."

Mac took the boy back to the house—to his home. Matthew was visibly shaken. He had lost his own parents first—now, he had to watch Kate be taken away in an ambulance—and Yeller—Mac didn't know what to do.

"Matthew? We have to wait here. They'll call. Waiting is the hardest part. Why don't we pray, Matthew? We'll call Sabrina and Nick—and Alexandra. They can pray with us. You can get on the extension phone, and talk to all of them."

It was the right thing to do. The child had a look of hope on his face when Mac suggested it. Mac left his cell phone on the table, in case the hospital, or the vet called them. He took the other phone that was in the house, and dialed the Stewarts' phone number. Matthew Clark needed his friends, right now.

"Lord, take care of John and Katie. Please let Dr. Martin and Maureen be there, since I can't," prayed Mac.

Chapter Twenty-Three

John Cabe sat in the waiting room of the Trauma Unit.

"How many times, Lord?" he prayed.

He watched, as Anthony Martin walked toward him.

"John, I'm so sorry. I just heard. I'm going in, right now."

"Dr. Martin? Save her. Please, save her."

Dr. Martin put his arm around John's shoulders and a sense of peace went through John Cabe.

"John, there's a Hospital Chapel just down the hall. Why don't you wait down there? I'll come and get you, as soon as you can be with her, again."

He didn't want to leave the area. At least, he was close to Kate where he was, but he did what the doctor had asked him to do. He walked into the small Chapel, and kneeled at the altar. He began to pray and he thought of Kate. He had seen her tonight—his sight restored—much as when he first found her. Why did she have to be hurt, again?

He looked up at the cross that was in front of him, and then glanced to the wall to his right. There—a painting caught his eye. He couldn't believe what he saw there!

There was an angel, a Saint, watching over a child, and animals. He looked at the name of the picture—"*St. Bridget of Ireland, Protector of Children and of Animals.*"

The angel's face in the painting was *Kate's* face...and the child? The child looked *exactly like Matthew!*

He didn't understand. What did this mean?

"John?"

He heard Maureen's voice behind him. As he turned, he saw her— a small middle aged, Irish woman. She didn't look like he thought she would, but she had a softness and a glow, that melted his heart.

"Maureen?" he asked.

"Yes, John. I'm Maureen. You can see me, can't you?"

"Yes, Maureen. I can finally see you. Did you hear about Kate?"

"That's why I'm here. I thought the two of us should pray together—agree that Kate will make it. I'm so sorry, John—that it had to be like this."

He collapsed into her arms, sobbing for Kate—for Matthew—even for the cat—and feeling only the warmth of Maureen's arms surrounding him.

"She's going to be all right, Matthew," promised Sabrina Stewart. "I talked to my angel, and she told me."

"You and that angel, Sabrina," said Matthew, as he gulped back a sob.

"Matthew, I'm surprised that you don't believe. Kate looks just like my angel. When I saw her in the hospital, I thought, 'Angel? Are you really Kate?' But, she told me she was some 'Saint'. She said that sometimes people see her when they look at other people. Didn't you see her, Matthew?"

"Well, I thought I did."

"And?"

"She looked a lot like my mom—my real Mom, Sabrina."

"That's okay, Matthew—at least you saw her, and so you know she's there. She's taking care of Kate, and Uncle Johnny. She's taking care of Yeller too, Matthew."

Matthew thought about it.

As they listened, Nick and Alex Stewart were weeping, not just for their friends, but also for these children.

Mac put his arms around Matthew.

"Nick? Alexandra? I'd like all of us to say a prayer, if that's okay?"

Alexandra Stewart remembered how happy they had been the last time she saw them—her best friend—and her newest friend. John and Kate were so happy. Thank God that John could see again. Surely, God wouldn't let that happen and then take away his whole world? She drew close to Nicholas—and he prayed—over the phone, for all of them.

Maureen went to see Dr. Martin. He was just coming from surgery.

"Is it over?" she asked.

"Yes. We've done everything that we could do."

"And, now?" she whispered.

"It's up to God—as it always is."

"Did she *see* you, Anthony?"

It was the first time that she had called him by his first name.

"She saw me, Maureen."

He smiled at her, as they walked down the hallway, past the Emergency Room and into the I.C.U. unit.

"Kate? Can you hear me?"

Kate Walcott's eyes fluttered. Had she dreamed of the tall man full of light? He had pulled her back, out of the darkness. She thought at first that it was Dr. Martin, but then she knew he was an angel.

Then, she saw Matthew and John waiting for her at the end of the light—such a bright, bright light! Kate knew that she had to get back to them. She had to fight.

"John?" she whispered.

As her eyes began to focus, she saw him—her husband.

"Hello, Beautiful," he said to her, tears filling his eyes.

"Oh, John—am I all right? Am I really here with you?"

Kate began to see him more clearly, as he drew closer to her, kissing her forehead.

"You're going to be all right, Kate. You're going to be fine, Love."

He tenderly kissed her hands, as he bent close to her face.

"Matthew? John, how's Matthew?"

"Matthew's going to be fine. Don't worry. Even our cat has at least one more life. Yeller's going to be okay too, Kate. I just spoke to Mac.

He held her hand even more tightly, and leaned down and kissed her face again.

"Kate? *You are beautiful*...what you did...how you look—I love you so much."

It was the way that he said it—"how you look." She touched his face and looked into his eyes. Then, she knew. He had his sight back—John could see her! Her prayers had been answered. Kate touched his eyes, and her hand fell to his mouth. He captured it, and kissed her hand.

"John, when? When did it happen?"

"When I found you, Kate—my darling—when I found you."

Although, he didn't see anyone but Kate, John Cabe felt a presence with both of them, as he sat there, beside her. He knew in his heart that Kate would be all right. He sat, just staring at her. She was so much more beautiful than he ever imagined. She was exactly as he envisioned the woman that he would spend the rest of his life with.

Epilogue

"She risked her life for Matthew," Dr. Martin said, looking down at Kate.

"A gift of love and sacrifice—for a child—and for an animal—just like the Saint that she was named for," whispered Maureen, "Katherine *Bridgett* Walcott Cabe."

"And he risked his life for her," smiled Anthony Martin, looking at John Cabe.

"Another gift of selflessness and courage—and so much *love*," smiled Maureen.

"And the boy? He risked his life for a friend," whispered Dr. Martin.

"A true gift of caring. His prayer for his family was answered, wasn't it?" Maureen asked him.

"His prayers, along with Sabrina's—those were the innocent faithful prayers of children, Maureen. He always hears them."

Anthony Martin smiled at her, "And, his parents and friends—what a circle of love, Maureen."

"Humans never cease to amaze me, Anthony."
"They're His most loved creation, Maureen."
"Amen, Doctor—Amen!"

THE END